On My Way to Someplace Else

On My Way to Someplace Else

Essays

Sandra Hurtes

Poetica Publishing Company

Printed in the United States of America 2009

Cover Photo:
Sandra Hurtes and her mother, Catskills Bungalow Colony, Summer, 1954

Cover Design:
Michal Mahgerefteh

Publisher:
Poetica Publishing Company
www.poeticapublishing.com
PO Box 11014
Norfolk, VA 23517

5.5" x 8.5"   144 pages
ISBN 978-1-61584-636-8 (ppb)

Order online at:
www.poeticapublishing.com
www.sandrahurtes.com

$15.00

Contents

In loving memory
of my parents

My mother and father in Prague, 1946

My father with his family on their shtetl in Lucket, Czech, 1937

My mother, three sisters and their mother
on their shtetl in Sasovo, Czech, 1940.

My mother, her brother and sister, 1946

My father, wounded in the army, with buddies

Thank you

Each essay in this book had readers. I thank every one, in particular, **Elyse Victor** who read every version of every essay. Her invaluable feedback and friendship has meant everything. **Joe Berman** gave me unlimited use of his office. I owe him a ton of printer paper and gratitude. I thank **Gretchen Fletcher** and **Deborah Baldwin** for many last-minute readings and suggestions; and my friends and family who encouraged my writing life from the start. I'm grateful to **Michal Mahgerefteh**, the publisher of *Poetica Magazine*, for her expertise and belief in this collection.

I often wished to rediscover within me the girl
who was innocent and full of knowledge
before they taught me what life was all about.

Liv Ullman, *Choices*

INTRODUCTION

The essays in this collection were written after I'd begun pondering a divide in myself, one separating me into two selves: a daughter of Holocaust survivors and an average, liberated American woman. Born in 1950 in Brooklyn, I was—at least on paper— American. But even as a young girl I understood that being American meant being lighter and freer than I often felt. I was a painfully self-conscious child, consumed with concern for my family's welfare.

The first piece in this collection is my first published essay. In it, I begin exploring my relationship with my mother—a gorgeous and painful presence in my life and a touchstone for much of my work—and the complex impact her Holocaust experiences had on me. This was the essay that helped me gain a third identity, as a writer. The rest touch on a range of themes. Some address the Holocaust; others spring from my experiences as the American Everywoman I've always longed to be. All are in some way about growing up, taking cues from society and peers, trying to make a life outside the life that had been ordained for me.

This collection contains my earliest essays. I offer them, believing that no matter how unusual my circumstances have been, they will resonate with anyone who has searched for an identity and found it in more than one place.

A Daughter's Legacy

The year, 1995, was the golden anniversary of my parents' liberation from concentration camps. Out of all the family stories my mother told me, the one firmest in my memory is that of the day of her liberation from Auschwitz.

My mother and her fellow prisoners woke up one morning in an eerily quiet bunk and knew by the silence that something had changed. They searched the barracks, looking for the SS, but instead of finding the guards they saw Russian soldiers running toward their camp, laughing and dancing wildly. The soldiers charged into the bunk and cried out joyfully, *"Te Svebodna"* {You're free}. A handsome soldier lifted my mother off her feet and although she was just skin and bones, he kissed her cheeks and told her she was beautiful.

When he put her down, she stumbled toward the open door. The women piled out, insane with joy. They ran from the barracks to the commissary, only to find the food sealed in cans, except for mustard, which my mother loved. She cupped her hands and drank the mustard like soup. Her stomach became distended. The others went outside and found a wagon hitched to a horse. They hollered, *"Rifka, mach schnell"* {hurry up}. She was rolling on the floor in pain. She believed she would die. The women carried her from the commissary and lifted her on to the wagon.

The barbed wire fence had been cut. The wagon crowded with women seemed to soar through the camp, down the dirt road. All along the roads were abandoned homes that the Germans had fled overnight. The women stopped and went into a house. They stripped the curtains off the windows. They tore their burlap uniforms off and wrapped the fabric around their bodies like sarongs, covered their bald heads with turbans.

In the Russian soldier's arms, and then again, wrapped in the chintz fabric, my mother reclaimed herself.

My mother was a beauty. When I was a toddler, as we made our way up and down Utica Avenue, we stopped at the butcher, the baker, the corner grocer. In each store keeper we "finagled" with, my mother found an avid audience. The effects of the war had left their mark on her, and her internal scars were not to be taken lightly. Yet she was a fascinating mix of radiance and sorrow. To the outside world my mother was an emblem: a heroic survivor who almost always wore a smile. But my youthful sensitivity and our close-knit relationship made me privy to the sadness hidden in her heart.

After her liberation, my mother had a reunion in Prague with her five sisters and brothers, who all miraculously survived the camps. But when she and my father married, his eldest sister, who was settled in Brooklyn, sponsored their voyage to America. My mother had to say good-bye to her siblings, who had no American sponsorship and emigrated instead to Israel.

Throughout my childhood I learned about my Israeli cousins through the endless stream of letters and pictures that traveled back and forth between our apartment in Brooklyn and their homes in Haifa and Tel Aviv. Whenever I saw the light blue envelopes edged with zigzag stripes in the mailbox, I knew I would lose my mother for a while, as she sat at the kitchen table, reading her letters through watery eyes and heavy sighs.

When she was finished with her letters she'd beckon me to her lap. We would sit together on her favorite chair in our apartment in Crown Heights, where she wove her tapestry of stories. She took me back to her childhood home in *Sasfala*, a *shtetl* in Czechoslovakia, up to her teen years when her mother died, and then to a place called Auschwitz and a man called Hitler. As I listened, I struggled with the mystery of how one person named Hitler could have killed so many people. My parents' one concession to modern life – the television – provided the answer.

Late Saturday afternoons my brother and I would sit in front of the Magnavox watching *Chiller Theater* on Channel 11. One evening it featured a movie called *The Attack of the Fifty Foot Woman.* As the giant woman stalked the city, crushing apartment buildings, cars, and throngs of people with one footstep, I then understood how Hitler could have done it. He was a fifty-foot giant!

When I was ten my parents took me to the Loew's on Pitkin Avenue to see a documentary that had actual footage of the war. It was called *Mein Kampf.* The pictures then became indelibly engraved in my mind. I would never forget the sight of bodies, skinnier than nails, heaped one on top of the other, among them even children. I loyally mourned for them and for all the lives that were no more.

I lay in my bed at night and thought about death and how it felt to walk into an oven big enough to hold people. I would hold my breath and wonder how it felt to be baked alive.

In 1961 when Adolpf Eichmann was captured, he became the victim of my silent rage. I plotted my revenge by picturing all the Jews in the world walking past him as he sat strapped in an electric chair. Each person would pass an electric current through him, but not enough power to kill him. He would sit there not knowing when his exact moment of death would come; only that it would.

I wanted Eichmann to suffer as my parents had, and my father's parents and four brothers who died, whose sweet, wet kisses I would never know.

As the world pays homage to the survivors of the Holocaust and commemorates the memory of those who died, I acknowledge that the legacy I carry as the child of survivors is a formidable one.

When I was growing up I desperately wanted to restore the happiness so bitterly stolen from my parents' lives. I was a good daughter and almost never made waves. I didn't want to cause them more pain then they'd already endured. Nor did I want to stir the guilty waters I tread whenever I did.

My parents wanted a life for me that held no sadness. But as they placed all their hopes and dreams for the future in my hands, they created a horrible dilemma for me—how would I ever separate from them when separation to them felt like grave loss and abandonment?   I couldn't, and for many years my parents' needs remained at the forefront of my life.

When I was in my mid 20's, I went through my first major crisis, a divorce. The painful situation forced me to look closely at myself for the first time. I realized that my bond with my parents was so tight, it had allowed no room for anyone else, not even my husband. My marriage hadn't stood a chance. I began then the very difficult process of separation. Perhaps because I got started late, or because of years of unspoken feelings being stored up, I did it with such a vengeance, that all parties concerned are still hoping I'll simmer down.

My anger at my parents frequently spills over, especially when I feel my own needs being submerged by the neediness I sense in them. For many years, I ran from the fear of being swallowed up by cutting all ties to them and by keeping everyone else a safe distance away. But I couldn't live without the closeness of others, and my need to have a relationship with my parents was extraordinary. I had to find another way.

One thing I had to do was let myself off the guilty hook. No matter how much love passes from myself to them, it could never be enough to heal their wounds. The only ones I can dress are my own; healing involves creating a life and finding my place in the world. This is my greatest challenge, especially as I make choices that move only my own life forward.

As I struggle to come to terms with the anger, guilt and love that I feel for my family, the worldwide attention the survivors are receiving has presented me with a wonderful opportunity. The public's compassionate viewpoint has enabled me to acknowledge the heroism inherent in my parents' survival and in their capacity to go on with their lives.

Like it or not, the Holocaust has been the binoculars through which I've viewed my life. Perhaps the greatest paradox of my legacy is that while I'm never without the foreboding knowledge that a life can be destroyed in a moment, I'm never without the hope of how magnificently that life can be reclaimed, restructured and relived.

*my mother referred to Sasovo as Sasfala

Paging Steven Spielberg

Like thousands of other Holocaust survivors, my mother has the opportunity to tell the Shoah Foundation the story of the years she spent in concentration camp. The organization, founded by Steven Spielberg, is archiving voluntary testimonies of all living survivors.

My mother was all set to be interviewed two years ago, having made arrangements with trained interviewers based in Florida where she lives. She telephoned me a few days before the interview to say she was too nervous to go through with it. I understood how the painful memories would upset her. But for most of my life, I'd heard her talk about how much she wanted to have her experiences documented. I tried to push her forward.

She phoned me again: "I'm too upset, and Daddy says not to do it."

Not knowing what to do, I acknowledged that as close to my mother's experience as I often feel, I had no idea what it would be like for her to "tell." Perhaps I should stay out of it, I thought, part of me grateful that my father stepped in—if, in fact, he really had—and made the decision for her.

She called me the next day to say she had canceled the appointment. That night, she phoned again to say she was sorry she had.

Now, two years later, my mother has reconsidered and is buoyed by the dream that she's started to nurse along. She says she's ready to talk—but only to the big *kahuna* himself, the man who brought Schindler back from the grave and erected him as a testament to the persistence of kindness in the midst of the most deplorable of human depravity. My mother wants to be interviewed by Steven Spielberg.

When she first told me, I found her wish charming and not surprising, since she has often dazzled others with her movie-star quality. My mother has always wanted to go Hollywood. The process began when after dyeing her hair from brunette to blond, she had an uncanny resemblance to the Gabors. Creating a stage for herself in the jewelry business she owned with my father, she *kibitzed* and shone so brightly that the bracelets and earrings she wore when she left the house in the morning were gone by evening, sold to customers who wanted to look just like her.

But the sadness camouflaged by her eyeshadow and hoop earrings made itself known behind the closed doors of our Brooklyn apartment. The story of my mother's life held me captive throughout my childhood and into young adulthood, until the day I was able to say to her, "I can't listen anymore."

As I moved away from my mother in order to find my own stage on which to shine, I dreamed about the future. My mother dreamed, too, about the life behind her and of one day telling that story to the world.

In many ways the Shoah Foundation would seem the perfect answer. Its compassionate interviewers, with knowledge of the sensitive issues, have the emotional distance needed to listen to the personal histories so full of horror. But to my mother, they lack the passionate response of family members so important to her.

For this reason, I saw her wish to speak to Steven Spielberg in another light and was struck by the significance. Giving so much power to a man she'd never met, believing that only he was qualified to hear her, made me think that perhaps she had unconsciously assigned to him a role neither he nor anyone else was qualified to play.

My mother's father died when she was three years old. While she was deeply loved by her three older brothers, I can't help imagining that, in some way, she has spent a great part of her life yearning for a father, especially one with the heroic capacity to heal the scars of Auschwitz.

Wanting to spare her the disappointment of finding out that Steven Spielberg, who unquestionably does appear so much larger than life, is but a mortal, I considered trying to persuade her it is more important that she tell her story than who she tell it to. I also realized that a meeting, even by telephone, would be no easy thing to pull off.

The more I thought about it, however, I realized that not only did I not have the right to determine the course of my mother's dreams, but also I couldn't blame her for wanting to walk into the heart of the man who so publicly opened his by insisting that the world remember. By fathering the Shoah Foundation, he provided a vehicle through which the survivors of the Holocaust could be validated and honored. My mother gleaned from that the hope that one day she might actually get to be heard by the entire world. Who better to turn to than the man behind it all, the man who, besides being so well connected, also just happens to seem like such a downright *mensch*?

My mother's wish makes more and more sense. I've decided to do my small part to help her—most openly by writing this essay, and most lovingly by not challenging her dream.

So, Mr. Spielberg, should you happen to read this while you're having your morning coffee and bagel, there's someone I know who would love a word or two—well, actually, more like a few hundred words with you. She's waiting for a call.

Keeping Alive The Dreams Of Love

It had been a long time since I'd met anyone promising in the romantic arena, and I'd pretty much retired the dreams I'd carried since childhood about marriage and children. I'd been settling instead for a sprinkling of dates, here and there, taking what I could get, almost forgetting that I'd ever wanted more.

One night on a whim I took myself out to a popular Manhattan dance spot where the lights were dim, the music loud, and the crowd lively. I sat at a small table surveying the scene when I spotted someone interesting across the dance floor. He looked at me, then looked away, and finally, he held my glance. Before I knew it we were playing the mating and waiting game, until the braver one of us stepped across the great divide and asked, simply, "Would you like to dance?"

We found our way easily into each other's rhythm, and to the tune of *This Can't Be Love*, we covered ground. As we dipped and twirled around the crowded dance floor, he whispered in my ear, "We have great dance compatibility." I heard in his words the hint of a future, and my cautious heart began to come out of hiding.

After dancing a few numbers we stopped to catch our breath, and over drinks we got acquainted.

"Do you take lessons?" he asked.

"No, but I'm thinking about it. Maybe West Coast Swing."

It seemed like the right thing to say, as if I was in the know. He told me about a new club in Soho, one that he was hoping to try. Then he got down to business. Taking out his wallet, he proudly showed me a picture of his son, "From an early marriage," he explained, quickly adding, "It's been over for years." I told him I'd been married once, also long ago, and I had no children. Pushing a ringlet back from my forehead, he asked me for my phone number. Then he wrote his own number on a scrap of paper, and his name in case I'd already forgotten. Richard.

We had our first date a week later. It was an easy evening with good conversation in a dark, crowded restaurant. Over shrimp curry and chicken tandoori, he told me about his good friend, Carol, with whom he often went dancing. She'd recently fallen in love, and he was hoping that would happen for him, too.

"I'd like to get married again and have at least one more child," he said as we walked outside, looking for a cab to send me home in. Standing on the corner not yet ready to part, I felt as if I was dreaming when he said he had told Carol about me.

"Let's call her and tell her how our date's going," he said, smiling.

When I got home that night I thought about how unusual it was to be with someone who was that open about what he wanted and so eager to involve me in his life. By our second date, his sincerity and lack of pretense were touching me in all the right ways, and my dusty old dreams for marriage and children were tumbling out of the closet.

"It would be nice to have a big family," he said on our third date, "because my parents died when I was so young."

My overbearing family seemed heavenly to him. I thought about inviting him for Thanksgiving to show him what the other side was really like. But I held back.

After dinner we went for a walk, and then we stood in front of my apartment building for a long time before he kissed me. As we walked inside we made plans for our next date. Dancing, we both agreed, at the club in Soho. It had a small dance floor, he'd heard. We'd have to go easy on the swirling. Bring it in a little closer.

The next day I thought about what I'd wear on our date and was looking forward to talking to Richard. I didn't hear from him for a few days though, which was a little odd, since we'd been speaking often. Finally, I called him at work but he wasn't there so I left a message. A little impatient, I also left a message on his tape at home. A few days later, still nothing. I was trying hard to keep my mind from going where it wanted to go—he lost interest, I was too eager, he got scared and ran. I found out soon enough it was none of the above.

Three days after our last date, Richard died in his sleep. It wasn't a heart attack, an aneurysm, or anything discernible. The autopsy report that came back eight weeks later was inconclusive but showed that it was of natural causes. I received a phone call from Richard's friend, Carol, exactly a week after our last date. She'd searched his house for my phone number and found it finally on his dresser. She was sorry she didn't get to me sooner, and no, there was nothing I could do. The funeral was already over, and so was *shiva*.

We hung up, and I sat very still waiting to feel something deep and dark inside, something that would move me to cry. But I felt nothing. No, I felt eerie. Why, I wondered, through the slow, steady shock that grew heavier, not lighter, as the days stretched into weeks. Why was I pulled in at the final hours to witness the end of a life I barely knew? What was the reason for us to meet?

Many months later I received my answer. I came home one evening from a date with a man I had started seeing. He was a divorced dad, not looking for a commitment, my usual scenario. As I reviewed my evening with this casual guy, I thought about how disappointed I was that he kept forgetting to show me pictures of his kids, and that he had to cut our night short because there was just too much he had to do the next day. Oh, and about next week, well he didn't know yet if he'd be available. He'd call me.

There was nothing to hope for with this new man, no fantasies to get lost in. It was all pretty dim. That's when I understood why I had to meet Richard. The feelings he stirred in me showed me my desire for love wasn't dead, just buried, and the dreams of my childhood still lingered in anticipation that they might yet come true. No, Richard wasn't taken from me to leave me hungry and wanting. He was given to me to show me the kind of life in which I had stopped believing.

I like to think that there was something special Richard got from me that he took with him to his final sleep. Perhaps he, too, experienced the sweet rush of old dreams resurrected and the wonder of living again in long, forgotten hope.

These exquisite treasures so many of us search for and never find, and maybe even worse, some of us no longer look. If that's true for you, then I'm here to tell you. Bringing a heart back to life can sometimes be so simple.

For me it all started with a look, a touch, and a dip on the dance floor.

AT ONE WITH HERSELF

After five tumultuous years in which I tried to turn the boy I
fell in love with into the man my parents wanted him to be, my
husband escaped into the night with a toothbrush and a warning:
"I'll be back for the stereo."

For the first nine days of his departure I would have taken
him back in a wink. The flow of pain showed me no mercy, reminding me of all the times I shouted at him, "I want a divorce."
The empty bed I crawled into each night, sagged with the weight
of my loss, the mirror I looked into laughed back in my face, "See
what you've done?" On the tenth day, however, my self-inflicted
torture came to a grinding halt.

When my husband first walked out, I wanted to believe that
I was better off without him, that the differences between us were
just too extreme. But I knew better. In trying to be my parents'
good daughter, I had allowed their expectations to become my
own. Rather than treasuring the differences in my husband, the
very reasons that I fell in love with him, I tried to extinguish them,
and make him someone my parents would be proud of.

Every Friday night I marched him over to their house for
Shabbos dinner even though what we really needed was to relax or
be with friends after a week of work. We spent the holidays with
my parents, adhering to their customs and rituals rather than defin-
ing our own. Even though I would often hear my mother's voice
escaping from my lips as I carried on about the shoes in the hallway, the socks on the floor, and the dishes in the sink, I couldn't
stop. Her criticisms were deeply embedded in me and became part

of my own angry barrage at the person closest to me, my husband.

Not that he was an angel. He had his faults, one of which was retreating to the bedroom for hours at a time to play the harmonica while listening to Leonard Cohen sing *Suzanne*. When his bad mood passed he would step into the living room and reject the record I was listening to, returning it to my pile of records, deemed "the bubble gum section."

"What's for dinner?" he would ask, while I did a slow burn like the Marlboro he lit up and left cooking in the ashtray. His worst fault, though, was that he tried too, to turn me into someone else. His style was flashy, and he wanted a woman who loved to party as much as he did. He was the last one to leave a good time, and I was the first one to point to my watch while yawning, "Can we leave yet?"

He played James Dean to my Pollyanna, and my untouched body was irrevocably awakened by his wandering hands, with their refusal to stop when I mouthed the word, no. His aggression, so different from my insecurity, had lured me like a magnet. Together we formed an apt complement. He released me from my sweet wholesomeness. I quenched his hunger for an anchor and a steady meal.

My mother enjoyed cooking for him, and before we married he was a regular at my family's dinner table. He loved to be the center of attention just like my mother, and when I was seated between the two of them, I juggled them as if they were balls in the air, making sure that each one got his or her share of the limelight.

The first time I shone brighter than either of them was on my wedding day. As I stood under the canopy, the Rabbi asked me if I took this man to be my husband. I looked at the man I was about to promise to spend my life with, and I started to laugh. Everyone in the temple laughed with me, but my soon-to-be husband scowled down at me and whispered, "You had to steal the show." He was right. On my wedding day I was sure of one thing—the only way I would get to have the spotlight was if I stole it.

In the five years we were together we visited many sins upon each other. Just when it looked like those sins had cost me everything I experienced the most honest moment of my life.

Ten days after my husband left, while I was cleaning I came across a miniature high-chair that a neighbor had thrown away. It seemed to reach out to me, and I brought it into my apartment, wondering what I could do with it. As I scrubbed the used and peeling high-chair, I thought perhaps I would place it in front of the windows in my living room and use it as a planter. I took down a spider plant that was hanging from the kitchen ceiling and placed it on the seat of the chair, spreading out the plant, so that the baby spiders hung over the sides, covering places where the paint had chipped away.

When I stepped back to look at my spontaneous creation, I realized it was the first independent step I had taken in my life. I overrode my mother's voice within me asking, "Who needs other people's garbage?" and my husband's saying, "Don't do anything without my say so."

It had been ten days since he left, and the insight into my relationship with my parents and husband had thrown me for a loop. My self-punishment was merciless, and the scotch I drank each night to blot out the pain didn't make a dent. But when I stepped back and admired my new planter and my first step towards making my home my own, the pain ceased, the scotch went back into the cabinet, and I began to breath.

A few weeks later, I returned home one evening from dinner out with a friend and found my husband waiting for me. He had a change of heart and was hoping I'd had the same. I sat down next to him and we held each other. I still loved him and wanted to take away his pain. As we sat together, wrapped in each other's comfort, I stared beyond him into the world that would be my future if I said, yes.

I saw myself at the end of my life, wondering what it would have been like if I had dared to take a chance and live a life for which I had no plan. I realized that just like that abandoned high chair had found a safe haven in my home, I could give that haven to myself.

I told my husband, no.

*

A few months after my husband and I separated, I went to Hawaii for a vacation, carrying a mixed bag of feelings with me onto the airplane. At times I was overwhelmed with sadness and questioned my decision to go forward with my divorce. Other times I was excited by the promise of the unknown, pumped up by an appreciative glance from a handsome stranger. Perhaps what was most disconcerting was the new awareness I had of myself.

All my life I believed that I would find my happiness in someone else and that by doing all the things I was supposed to, I would be protected from life's pain. I was a good daughter, and I tried during my marriage to stay involved in my family's life. That was what I learned when I watched my cousins marry and leave home, and it was what my mother longed for when she spoke to me of her friends.

"What a good daughter Shirley is," she'd say to me when she saw her friend Esther walking arm in arm with her daughter, pushing the baby carriage that held her first-born grandchild. "Susie is so close to her parents," my mother said when her friends Helen and Abe went on a vacation with their daughter and son-in-law. The comparisons to other people's children started when I was a child, and molded me into becoming someone who longed to be someone else.

One day while rummaging through a box of old photographs with my mother, I came upon a familiar snapshot taken of her many years before, holding the hand of a little girl. It's a gorgeous picture of the two of them, the child's smile, wide as the moon. Whenever I looked at that picture I would feel a stab in my heart and long to be that child.

"Who is this girl?" I asked my mother after so many years of wondering.

As she looked at me with utter confusion, I suddenly saw what I never could before. That girl was me. It was so evident in the knocked knees and familiar play suit that my mother sewed for me, and yet it was a shock. I already was the person I longed to be.

I wish I knew that when I stood under the canopy as a young bride laughing, and again, when I walked out of the honeymoon suite and into my own life. Knowing would have made all the difference.

SAME LIFE, NEW CONTEXT

Since the World Trade Center tragedy, I move through my apartment in a strange state of paralysis and anxiety. Nothing feels right. Joe, the man I'm dating, left a long, depressing message on my answering machine the other day. Something about his job, a long wait at the airport—the stuff of life—not war. I asked him not to leave me long, depressing messages. He said he'll only call me when he's feeling cheerful.

Our relationship has been a lot of struggle. Joe reminds me of my father. My father used to leave me messages in a sad voice, foggy with need and fear—"Where are you?" "Call me." "Please." Terrorists weren't attacking us then. He and my mother are always seconds away from running for cover.

In the streets, I look at missing-persons photographs tacked to trees—husbands, fathers, sisters, mothers, sons, daughters— with headlines asking, "Have you seen this person?" This painful searching for survivors, so primal and desperate, takes me back to my parents' past. I see myself in the *shtetl* as I imagine it, next to my mother who is seated on a bench in a torn dress with dirt smudges on her face. I feel primitive, of the earth, cloaked in other people's grief.

Joe was mad. "I should be able to turn to you when I feel bad." That's what he said. "You're supposed to be my sparkle, not bring me down," I countered. Silence. I put the issue on the shelf along with other things about Joe that make me unsure. I'm not ready to decide. The events of the past weeks are revising me too quickly. I don't know who I'll be tomorrow.

In the 1970's I was living with a hippie. He wore his wavy, chestnut hair in a ponytail, with a two-inch wide band around his forehead, sort of like Pocahontas without the feather. Our apartment reeked of marijuana and incense. Whenever I see a shag rug, that musky, claustrophobic scent comes back to me, as I recall the roaches (not the kind you step on) lodged in the rug's design of a blazing forest. We wore peace signs then on chains around our necks, and laughed at Nixon flashing the peace sign on his fingers. *Peace, peace be with you, go in peace, give peace a chance.*

When we broke up, my hippie wanted to live in a tepee in Poughkeepsie. He was running from nuclear war and relationship combat. From his profile he looked like an ax murderer.

I dreamt about him last night. He was having sex with my friend (in real life, she'd never), and I couldn't stop them because I was trapped in the caverns of the Twin Towers.

I'm lost in the past, yet I'm here today. I'm sitting at my computer. It's 11:35 a.m., the sun is shining in my living room windows, and I know exactly where I am. I'm not lost. My friend calls and asks if I want to go shopping for gas masks. We joke about keeping a backpack by the door filled with necessities in case we have to evacuate at the last minute.

Two paperbacks
A journal
Pens
Water
Pretzels
Prozac.

Prozac Packs. A modicum of control over a world gone haywire. Three thousand people died, among them my friend's husband, W. Last July when a bunch of us met for a high school reunion, she showed us his picture and emphasized, "He's so stable." She glowed. "Stable" is what everyone said about him when they talked at his memorial.

I'm ashamed to admit that I saw the Twin Towers for twenty years from my window, but I've already forgotten where they stood. I never met W. But I know where he stood—close to his wife and family—he was a family man, a regular guy, the kind you'd turn to in a fire and believe that he could save you.

I close my eyes often and try imagining his death. Had it been me, I pray I would've passed out or gone insane, just before I burned.

Get on with life, everyone says. Forget the news. Good advice—I started my day with a trashy news daily, and it's been downhill every since. Go to yoga or do aerobics. Buy flowers and forget the gas mask.

Joe told me yesterday he feels as if he's always doing the wrong thing. I told him that's because he is. He didn't laugh. Maybe he keeps things on a shelf too, all the things about me that make him unsure.

I'm scared—I'm on fast forward, although every day since September 11 feels like a year. Joe wants to know where I see us going. *I don't know.* My inner landscape has changed. The Holocaust defined me even before I was born. I've lived each day anticipating disaster, but when disaster flew close to my home, en route to the World Trade Center, it passed me by.

Where were you when the Twin Towers were hit? The question of the new millennium. This is where I was: watching, praying, crying, all the while thinking—my entire life has been a sham. Tragedy *isn't* ear marked for me any more than it is for anyone else. *What an epiphany.*

Late last night I thought I heard my phone ring, something that usually shakes me to the core. Adrenaline didn't pump through my body. I lay there and wondered, where do I go from here?

Pondering The Biological Clock's Tick
(or, the baby issue #1)

I grew up believing that one day I'd be a mom. When I was a young girl I dreamed of motherhood as I played with my dolls, and then later when I graduated to babysitting. I was taught that through a husband and children I would find my happiness. When I married at twenty I looked forward to one day being the mother of three!

My maternal desires at that stage were about living out the dream life portrayed on television and bringing my parents the greatest joy: grandchildren. My parents viewed my brother and me as the completion of their lives. So when I left their home to marry, they told me they filled their void with the hope of being grandparents.

During that time the women's movement entered my consciousness challenging my old-fashioned upbringing. I questioned my traditional roles, both as passive wife and loyal daughter. My husband had tried to free me from my deep bond with my parents, yet, he, too, resisted my liberation. *If I knew I'd have to do housework, I would never have married you.*

As our marriage unraveled, I considered having a baby as a way of holding on to the only life I knew. A baby or a divorce—it would be one or the other. It was the other, and after five years together we separated.

At 25 I had the rebellion that most people go through in their teens. I turned against everything I believed in by eschewing marriage and motherhood, and trying, finally, to separate from my parents.

But, I was overwhelmed by my choices; and so, instead of moving forward I went backwards for awhile by giving to myself experiences I'd sidestepped by marrying so young.

To sow my wild oats I spent more time on a plane then on the ground. I went to Club Med to see what the hoopla was all about. Then I packed a knapsack and traveled on my own through Europe the way my friends had when they were 18. At 29 I went to college.

When I took on my first serious endeavor, getting my degree, my childhood dream to marry and have children reared its head. The entire time I was in school I nursed serious husband and baby dreams, looking at my professors as potential mates, interpreting a scribbled "see me" at the bottom of a term paper as a possible request for a date. I was a girl in a woman's body, flirting, experimenting and learning about life, not necessarily through my books.

Then, in the midst of my studies, I resurrected a childhood hobby. I started a hand-knit sweater business specializing in infant sizes. Surrounded by all those baby clothes I felt comforted, but it wasn't the way I hoped to make my mark, through a talent I inherited from my mother. When I graduated, I chose a career in publishing.

By my mid-30s I settled into myself. I was happy as an editor and had made lots of friends at work. I felt attractive and full of life. But the ticking of my biological clock grew loud as women all around me, both married and single, were getting pregnant. I grew dizzy with baby fever, and as the sickness took hold I couldn't look at a man—any man—without checking his ring finger. When someone took my phone number, I would have us married with children before our first date. If I was really attracted to him, I would stand in front of my mirror with a pillow under my blouse, dreaming of happily ever after.

In all my fantasies of motherhood I had a daughter, and I was doing for this daughter what my mother couldn't do for me— giving her an identity beyond the home and a push out the door.

Concerned that I might never find someone to have a child with, I surveyed my male friends to see if any of them would impregnent me. A longtime friend made a pact with me—if we were both still available at 40 we would have a child together. A former boyfriend, one who had a vasectomy, volunteered to have his operation reversed if it came to that. I tucked my offers away like money in the bank.

But when I turned 40, instead of being haunted by the ghosts of my unborn children as I feared I would be, I was relieved that having a baby, at least a biological one, would soon no longer be an option. I began enjoying my relationships with men more, no longer secretly wondering if they would be the father of my child. As 42 and 43 crept up I saw that the way my life was playing out, single with no children, was the way it would be. I also saw that not having children was as much out of choice as chance.

Much of my adulthood has been about giving myself the things I missed in my childhood—a wide array of choice, the belief that I could be whoever I wanted to be and an arena in which to experiment. As much as I wanted children at various stages of my life, I wanted something else more—never to feel held back again by somebody else's agenda. So I gave myself the things that were most important and the truest to what I needed. I didn't know if this would always feel right. But it was the best I could do at the time.

As my biological clock sounds its final hurrah, I feel a mixture of panic and relief. It's hard to stop believing that a baby will complete my life, and I still want to bring my parents a grandchild. But I'm told by those who know that motherhood is nothing like what I imagine it to be, that it's an adventure into the unknown. I'm not afraid of treading unknown waters.

The thing is, I finally like knowing where I'm going.

Reduced Expectations

After watching the Academy Awards I decided to go off my diet. Looking at actresses who earn enough money to feed entire nations, yet appear emaciated and in desperate need of a good meal, sent me charging to the fridge. That's not to say I wouldn't like to be a size two and wear a clingy dress like Uma or Hilary. I have been as thin as they are, and the truth is, once the novelty wore off, I wasn't any happier than I am right now.

I've spent over one-half of my life concerned about my weight. The eternal ten pounds that I mull over in my mind, for a minute here, a minute there, add up to a nice chunk of time that I could be thinking about far meatier issues - raising money for AIDS research, housing the homeless, my next article. But with the self-centeredness of the body-obsessed, the scale in my mind never sleeps. While waiting for a train, attending a business meeting, or sitting at my computer, a voice inside my head comes out of nowhere, and tells me, "I'm so fat."

In the movie *Sex, Lies and Videotape,* Andie MacDowell's character tells her therapist that women would be fat and happy if there were no men in the world. Although all the women in the audience laughed in acknowledgment, I don't believe women's weight is a simple female/male issue. I've never been with a man who thought I needed to lose ten pounds. Still, I wage a daily war with myself equating sexuality with being thin, and I dole out self acceptance with how closely I weigh in.

When the television program *Melrose Place* was on the air, I wanted to send the show's female stars a care package. They were scarily skinny. Was I jealous? Yes. But I was angry too. Although I knew better than to let the media define me, the messages fed into what I've been taught ever since I began to care about how I look. If Heather Locklear, a size 2, had a different man every week begging her for sex, somewhere inside me I believed that if I was ever to have sex again, I had to look, at least from the back, like a pubescent girl. So during commercials, instead of writing a letter of complaint to producer Aaron Spelling, I was on the floor doing sit-ups.

Don't get me wrong. I'm not opposed to healthful living. It's just that often the true meaning of "healthy" gets blurred. Especially by me. Several years ago I went to a Palm Springs health spa for a vacation. Comfortable with my weight, I didn't go there for the dieting but to relax in a place I'd never before been.

After three days, however, I got caught up in the low-calorie meals and strenuous exercise and the effect they were having on my body. I loved it, believing I was only in it for the week. But upon returning home, something strange happened. I couldn't start my day without a bowl of Shredded Wheat, couldn't even look at "fattening" food, and the early morning hikes I enjoyed so much, translated in city terms to walking everywhere, forget about subways.

After a month of continuous diet and exercise the pounds began to fall off. I was in awe of the process and loved getting skinny. Three months later, I was two sizes smaller, and my hip bones stuck out prominently enough that I could see them through my clothes. What a rush!

I looked good. Although some friends thought I was too thin, I felt fit and was eating well. Sounds great. The problem was that all I thought about was food. What I would eat for my next meal. What I wasn't eating. What other people were eating that they shouldn't be. How many miles I would walk the next day to work off the extra bites of something I wished I hadn't swallowed. I wasn't aware of the treadmill I was on until I ran into a friend I hadn't seen in a long time, and she asked me how my summer was. I realized that the only pleasure I had during those leisurely months was showing off my new body in skimpy clothes. A day at the beach didn't mean fun; it meant comparing myself to other women. It felt a little crazy and dangerously close to anorexia.

I loosened my grip on myself, and my weight went up a bit. It was around that time that Oprah Winfrey was often in the news for her weight-loss ups and downs. I knew what her problem was. She'd taken off too much weight and couldn't maintain such uber-thinness. She needed to accept the weight that was right for her body.

Now she seems to have found her way. But, have I found mine? I've gained a few pounds. This is an indicator that I love to eat and get great pleasure from food. I'm not skinny anymore, but I'm not overweight. Can I leave myself alone?

I'm trying. I went shopping for clothes the other day. Browsing through the store, I caught a glimpse of myself in the mirror, and what I saw upset me. It wasn't my body, but the way I was dressed. Long flannel shirt, baggy pants—a woman in hiding. I rummaged through the racks and found something black, sexy, with a little cling. I bought it.

This body acceptance thing is going to take time, and I can't do it alone. You see, when I was shopping I noticed an interesting phenomenon. Women's clothes start at size zero. How low can we possibly go? Before starving into nonexistence, it's time to stop and think about something. Is this the change that we've been fighting for—to be heard but not seen?

My Daughter/My Self
(or, the baby issue #2)

My daughter is running through the store, trying on hats and vamping it up. She's modeling for me and charming everyone who is watching her. What a delicious sight she is.

Later, I drop her at ballet class. Before I make my exit, I peek through the curtain at her small, lithesome body, and watch her face, serious and intent as she *plies*. She sees me. I disappear.

While sitting at the counter at a coffee shop on Manhattan's Upper West Side, I look at my watch and remember where I am. I'm ten minutes late for my therapy session—there she is again—my fantasy daughter holds me up while she delights my brain.

"Are you longing for your childhood?" my therapist asks when I tell her how I stare at children in the street, hug them with my eyes and cleave to the sound of their froggy voices. Do I want to be their mom, I wonder, pulling myself away to do the next grownup thing I've got scheduled for my day, or do I want to crawl inside their skin and become them? It's hard to know.

I return to Jesse, my make-believe daughter, for clues. Almost always she's my all-American girl. I never tell her of her grandparents' history. I wrap her in gauze and shield her in a protective cocoon. She'll never watch black-and-white film clips of skeletal bodies, learn of the deaths of my father's family members, or see the yearning that begs forth from my parents' eyes. I don't want my daughter to know the pain of being asked to complete another person's life and the futility of failing at such an impossible task.

Other times Jesse is the bridge between my parents and myself, my peace offering. A generation apart, with me as buffer, Jesse gives my mother the attention she so hungrily craves and takes in the good stuff that our cultural differences bear. My mother woos her granddaughter with her Zsa Zsa-like charms. She tells her my favorite childhood story, *"The Chadala Babala,"* a sort of Hansel and Gretel, and my mother bumps fists with Jesse as they play *etzem petzem picolara*, one potato two. My mother's on good behavior. I've allowed her into my daughter's life, but only under the condition that she never tell her about her past. She loves her granddaughter passionately, and she knows I mean business. She obeys.

As a single woman with no children, the winding down of my ability to have a biological child has lowered the curtain on a wish I've held since young adulthood—to raise a child untouched by the scars of the Holocaust. A fantasy child is frozen in my mind at the age of seven. She has long brown curly hair, an agile body and a curiosity that pushes her beyond all hesitation. Like me, she is American-born. Unlike me, she isn't first generation. This is my gift to her—a history that isn't laced with pain; a present unencumbered by differences. My American birth is the most profound way in which I define myself as different from my mother. Yet my wish to connect with my mother is a shadow that has followed me my entire life.

Years ago, before her arthritic bones and unsteady heart rhythm caused her and my father to move to Florida, while she was still skirting the fringes of her prime, I'd walk in the street and sometimes hear the thick accent, so reminiscent of her, falling from the lips of other ladies. They were fancy ladies—Hungarian, with rich black hair or golden blond, trilling their *r*'s, speaking animatedly. I'd stand up close, inhaling their Chanel, and become filled with longing. Later, heart in hand, I'd stand by the telephone wanting to call my mother, wondering which mom would I get—the one whose sadness blankets me, or the good mom, the one Jesse knows?

She'd read my mind and call me first. *"Simala"* she'd breathe into the phone, my Hebrew name, little *Sima. "It's mommy. I vanted to hear your woice.*" My heart would catch as my feelings tilted like a seesaw.

Unlike many survivors who told their children little about the camps or their pre-war lives, my mother wove endless stories. In this regard our relationship was different from those of many other daughters and their survivor mothers.

My mother told me of the brutality of the SS who tore into the female inmates searching for hidden wealth in the most intimate places, the line-ups where she stood with her sisters while the SS chose who went to death and who was worth saving for labor, and her loneliness for her own mother, which presented itself as an inability to tolerate any kind of separation.

My father spoke seldom about the war. At times he appeared to be like a wounded sparrow, and whenever I caught a glimpse of him from the back I was reminded of his pain. Beneath his left shoulder blade is a six-by-three-inch banana-shaped scar, the result of a bullet wound he received while serving as a paratrooper in the army. Every evening the scar announced itself to me as he leaned bare-chested into the Yiddish newspaper, his shoulders hunched in a self-effacing repose.

In my late-20s I'd entered therapy to explore the breakdown of my marriage. My mother's phone calls had cracked through the tender fiber of my relationship with my husband, and I'd struggled to understand to whom to give my loyalty.

I'd chosen a man whose tie to his own parents was flimsy. Maybe unconsciously I believed he wouldn't threaten my own familial tie, or perhaps I saw a sense of freedom in him that I couldn't find within myself. But my ambivalence about my marriage kept me in a state of limbo.

When my marriage ended I was filled with guilt over its dissolution, but my relationship with my husband received little attention during my therapy sessions. I hadn't yet learned how deeply my father's quiet had affected me. And so it was the content of my mother's conversations that ate up my first six months on the analytic couch. They filled my therapist's office with a ghostlike echo, so that I'd hear her voice the way I'd heard it when I was three years old, singing, *"Que sera, sera, what will be will be,"* as she dusted and mopped or pushed a brush through my thick curls. The bittersweet lilting of her voice wrapped around me as I talked to my therapist. I felt the imprint of her head on my shoulder, recalled my fingers tapping her on the back the way she'd taught me. Soft touches, like rat-a-tat-tat.

"My little Goldilocks," she'd say when she lifted her head from my shoulder. "*Simala*, you're my reason."

"I made a mistake," my mother would respond at times, when I'd tell her how she'd overwhelmed me when I was young. "I shouldn't have told you about the camps," she'd say.

Other times she couldn't understand my refusal to continue listening. Orphaned at 15, her longing for her mother was so deep, she had created a memory of her that was of heroic proportion.

"As long as your mother is around ...," she'd admonish me, shaking her fist, unable to grasp how I no longer felt as she did, that a mother's life should be everything to her daughter.

After my divorce I chose a life the total opposite of the one I'd been raised for—or perhaps it chose me—single, childless, a life that would feed only myself. My mother's stories lessened, but her sadness still leaked into me. Her loneliness lived in her voice, wavy with anxiety. In therapy I'd tried to learn how to distance emotionally from my mother's voice. But where therapy was a powerful microscope, it was a very weak weapon. I failed abysmally where it really counted—making that separation.

When my mother telephoned, my skin would tighten across my chest as I braced myself to hear something painful. If she said she was depressed or sad, it could destroy my happiness for the next week. Should I go to her? I'd wonder on my way to meet friends for a movie or dinner. Sometimes I'd slip away and call to see how she was doing. When I did, I'd later become consumed with anger. If I didn't I was filled with guilt.

And so much shame. None of my friends were as consumed by their mothers as I was by mine.

"Don't call me so much," I'd beg.

"*Vat did I do wrong?*" she would ask.

Three weeks would go by without a word. Life felt normal, even keel. I was like my peers, able to think about myself and move my own life forward. Then one of us would buckle.

"*Ve miss you*," my mother would say, and my heart would cave because I missed them, too.

Sometimes the phone call would be fleeting, a hello or fragments of thoughts about "touchy" subjects. Was I dating anyone special? Did I have enough money? When was I coming for a visit.

"Yes, yes, and I don't know," I'd offer. Careful not to mention anything that would induce attention, like I had a scratchy throat or something in my apartment was broken, sometimes I'd slip and say I had to get to the supermarket before it closed.

"Vat do you need?" she'd ask.

"Just a few things—soda, tuna, milk."

"Should Daddy bring it?"

"Daddy?" My skin would prickle. "The store is on the corner." Before moving to Florida, my parents lived a forty-minute drive away, yet my father once called to say he wanted to come over to bring me a *TV Guide* because he accidentally bought two. It could break my father's heart to withhold a way for him to fix my life. A *TV Guide*, milk, even a nickel, could do it.

A week later, a case of Seven-up would arrive at my door with twenty cans of tuna fish pulled off the shelves of their pantry. A nightgown, six pairs of panty hose and a brown, vinyl change purse with a twenty would be thrown in. On top was always the same note, written phonetically, in thin, harsh pen strokes—*Ve luv yu. Buy yurself somting.* I'd look through the hallway and down the stairwell—if she remembered I needed milk, surely there was a cow somewhere.

Sometimes the packages were discreet. I'd come home from work and find in my mail, jiffy bags stuffed so full they were torn and the gray stuffing was falling out. The packages appeared frail and desperate, and *shtetl* life appeared before my eyes. I'd stand in front of the incinerator late at night, dropping lipsticks that weren't my color, and nightgowns in little-girl styles down the chute. Occasionally there'd be a dress or knickknack that I loved, and I was stumped. Keeping it felt like I was in cahoots with thieves who were trying to steal my life. Throwing it away meant robbing myself of the good stuff. My hand would hover over the chute dangling a dress, distraught, maniacal.

To my friends it was funny, even poignant. Palms outstretched, they'd offer to take what I didn't want. But the gifts didn't mean the same to them. When they saw the penmanship, like a childlike scrawl, they didn't feel their lives being pulled, or see my parents in their mind's eye, moving rapidly through their kitchen shelves with such purpose, as if they had waited all day for something to do.

Finally I thought of a way to change my mother's tempo. I remembered the ladies on the street wrapped in mink and perfume, and I became one of them.

"*Avichka,*" I'd say loudly into the phone, her Hungarian name, mimicking her accent as I strung together the few Hungarian words I knew, into a sentence.

"Yes, darling," she'd sing, the need evaporating from her voice. We'd talk about shopping and make-up, gossip about friends and relatives, and we'd laugh like crazy. It was a relief to be freed from the confines of the mother/daughter roles we'd been dealt. Had we been two strangers who'd just met we could have been friends. Today, my mother holds court at her condo with all the daughters who fly down to visit their parents.

Two of these daughters have called me when they've come to New York and were stunned to learn that my relationship with my mother is so fraught with conflict.

"She's the most beautiful woman I've ever met," one said to me. "I talk to her for hours. She's my other mother."

My mother sits on the beach, her tanned skin glistening with *Bain de Soleil,* reading Louise Hay's books on personal growth. As she walks in the shallow part of the ocean with these borrowed daughters, she tells them how she's trying to heal her life. It can be mesmerizing to listen to her, to look at her face, eyes shining with tears always at the ready. A radiant survivor with a light in her eyes and a sorrow in her smile, she's an attention grabber— Zsa Zsa Gabor with an edge. She has a tragic past that no one can fault her for, except, shamefully, her own daughter.

If I'd been a mother, could I have raised my daughter outside the circle of my own pain? Many children of survivors who grew up not knowing the intimate details of their parents' experiences, feel excluded from their legacy.

Maybe my daughter would have pointed a finger demanding to know who I really am. Or would she have thanked me for stepping aside and giving her the room in which to grow? If so, I wonder if that would have felt like a coup or the painful stirring of an old wound.

I often felt pale and insignificant next to my mother. My blue jeans, Brooklyn accent and bangs that swept my eyes horrified her.

She'd survived a childhood of poverty, the early deaths of her parents, and Auschwitz, yet my American ways threatened to do her in. What could she have seen when she looked at me? Memories of her own teenage years walking barefoot in the snow, or a multitude of possibilities she needed to control because she knew how low the outside world could go?

My mother sent in the troops to get my love. But I could never repay her for giving me the things I didn't want. My only way out felt like turning my life back in time, fulfilling what would have been my most profound success: delivering a grandchild to her door. It wasn't that I didn't want to get married again and have a baby. I just didn't have the energy to make it happen, except for in my fantasies, the land where what I wished for could come true.

Flying my make-believe daughter to Florida, I watch as my mother basks in her presence. Symbol of the blood that Hitler couldn't suck, Jesse is a dagger in his heart. For this alone she receives the royal treatment. She lounges poolside on a beach chair while my mother gives her a manicure and pedicure, pink polish in her palm, humming a song. Like the Pied Piper, my mother is surrounded by other women's children. She's in heaven with these beings who accept her love, winking at Jesse, letting her know that she's her special girl. Before bedtime my father goes out to buy her a chocolate frappé, while my mother does her hair up in a French braid.

Armed with instructions as to what they cannot discuss, they protect Jesse from their history. Maybe she will learn about the Holocaust in school, a few steps removed in the way textbooks generally are. Perhaps she'll learn about it in Hebrew school. It hasn't quite been determined what her Jewish education will be. What is for certain is this—she will be a psychologically healthy child.

Not afraid to make waves.
Not afraid to stand up to me.
Not afraid.

At the eleventh hour my maternal cravings leap out at me. I want a child. A chance to do it different. Or do I want to recreate myself? My biological clock sounds its final wake-up cry. I hear it, but still I sleep.

And dream.

Playing Chase, Capturing A Heart

Like all families, Ben and I have our rituals. And in a world where families come in all shapes and sizes and often have nothing to do with blood, we're entwined by time, a mutual love for his parents and the unspoken understanding that when our eyes meet and a smile curls our lips, that means only one thing. We're off and running.

It all began when Ben started crawling. There he was in his corduroy overalls, working his way around the family room sofa, each inch a major victory. I watched him curiously, when he looked up at me, smiled and challenged me with his huge brown eyes. And so began the chase.

"I'm gonna get you," I said, sprinting around the sofa, while Ben tunneled beneath the coffee table. After about 30 seconds I reached down, grabbed him and said, "I got you!" He broke into peals of laughter. I don't know what was more pleasurable, his joy, or the fact that I'd found a way to wrap my arms around his normally squirmy body, which slid out of everyone's hug but his mom and dad's.

The next time I stopped by to visit with Ben's mom, she and I sat at the dining room table chatting and sipping coffee, when he crawled up close to me. Thinking he wanted to sit on my lap, I reached down for him, only to grab two handfuls of air. He'd turned and taken off, with a quick look back to see if I was following. Off I went, leaving his mom midsentence.

When Ben started walking, the chase became more involved. He took off for the hallway, went up and down the stairs, into closets and under beds.

"Where is Ben?" I'd ask, standing only a millimeter away, looking around, and his nervous giggle barely audible. I'd wait a beat, then look down, touch a toe or finger, and his laughter poured through the apartment. One day, his mom filmed us. Ben named the video, *The Sandy Show*.

Not being a mother, I sometimes feel an ache inside when I see a mom teaching her son or daughter valuable lessons. I want to be part of a similar cycle, leaving behind something as precious as a child who is happier, smarter or kinder because of something I did. Then I remember the effect a cousin had on me when I was growing up, and I know that love, like families, isn't one-size-fits-all.

As a painfully shy five-year old, I dreaded visiting relatives. But among my best memories are visits to Philadelphia, where my grown-up cousin Al lived. My mother, brother and I arrived mid-day Friday, while Al was at work. When it grew dark outside, I'd stand at the head of the staircase listening for the sound of his key turning in the door, preparing for our ritual.

"Al's home!" my aunt would announce when she saw his silhouette behind the door. I'd laugh, posing for a few seconds, then walk down the steps gingerly, knowing he'd scoop me up when I got to the first-floor landing, smile and announce, "Gorgeous is here!"

The act continued all through my not-so-wonder years of prepubescent gawkiness, adolescent acne and teenage insecurity, making me feel for that time that I was his entire world.

It has been many years since then, with lots of life's lessons—good and bad—steeped on top of that memory. But each time I turn from wallflower at the party to a woman with a full dance card, I know it's due in large part to my connection to a man other than my father who loved me unconditionally not because I was his, but just because.

When Ben was six, he and his parents left the city for the suburbs of New Jersey. As his life changed, so did he. There were rules: "Don't call me "Sweetheart." "No hugs!" Throughout his maturing, though, the chase prevailed, getting more daring as we raced around the spacious house with its expansive lawn, trees, winding driveways, finished basement and umpteen closets for hiding.

Ben is now nine. He's slender and agile and he gives me a good workout when we play chase. When I showed up last weekend, I brought running shoes. Just before leaving I said, "Ready to chase?" He smiled and nodded, adding, "This may be our last."

I'd known it was coming, hadn't expected the game to last as long as it had. His mom shot me a knowing look, and then I laced up my sneakers, and set out to make the chase a good one. I ran after Ben, then we switched midstream and he ran after me, then we switched again with neither of us getting tagged and went on like that until coming to a standstill: Ben in front of the sofa, me behind it, no one budging. The clock ticked. His mom washed dishes in the kitchen. The television hummed in the family room. We were silent as we stared each other down. Ben looked away. I swooped in to grab his arm, but he caught mine instead. His laughter spilled through the house.

That sound is an echo I'll hear forever, reminding me of the bond Ben and I forged. It's also an acknowledgement that I have given something to a child—different from what his parents give, but no less valuable. Just as my cousin Al responded to a need in me and acted on it, I saw that gleam in Ben's eye and ran with it.

A Quiet Ache

When I visited my father who was one week out of hip surgery, the hesitancy I inherited from him was nowhere in sight.

"Watch me, Sandy," he called out proudly. "I'm on all fours."

He was gliding around the fourth floor of Hollywood Memorial Hospital with his walker. His nurse, standing by in starched white, softened at the sight of him. His physical therapist mirrored back the smile I've known my whole life, lips closed but turned slightly upward, complacent as a tired, old cat. My eyes watered as he headed back toward me.

"Why are you crying?" he asked, his eyes starting to fill up too. "At the condo we call these Cadillacs."

As I watched my father take his post-surgery steps, so childlike and earnest, the fragility of his life hit me hard, although it has never been more than a whisper away. A survivor who lost half his family, my father's quiet ache is my own wound. In my strongest childhood recollection I see him sitting bare-chested at the kitchen table in our Crown Heights apartment, the Yiddish newspaper opened on his lap.

The scar on his back from a bullet wound, symbolized his quiet and solitary mourning, deeply dug into the skin, crudely healed over by flesh that looked like a third-degree burn. When I was a child I believed my father was reading the newspaper searching for information about his youngest brother, David, whose death during the war was never documented. But when I was older I discovered my father's search was far more inclusive.

The guttural sounds echoing off the Yiddish newsprint transported him back to the world of his own childhood so that he saw in his mind's eye: Hebrew books leaning on a bookcase made from rough planks of wood. *Shabbos* candles burning hotly atop the stove. His mother waving her arms over them as she prayed, a lace shawl covering her coarse black hair streaked with thin strands of gray.

In America, my father tried to recreate this world in my brother and me. But the two of us, so different we were termed "night" and "day," were acutely united in our refusal to be Europeanized and our ambivalence about Judaism. After eight years of a yeshiva education, my brother sloughed off his Hebrew books as if shaking free of an atomic bomb. He hated being a yeshiva boy. But when he began a quest for meaning in his life it was to Israel he turned. Life on a kibbutz gave him a peace he'd never before known.

As a girl, I was allowed to attend public school. My assimilation into American culture was easier than my brother's, and I assuaged my guilt by hating the Rabbis with him. But in the back of my mind I nursed the feeling that had I been a yeshiva girl I would have filled the emptiness in my father's heart that my brother couldn't, and I looked at boys in yarmulkes and girls in white knee socks through a strained cloth of shame and sadness.

My father's quiet ache was louder than the myriad stories I'd heard on my mother's knee of her own wartime experiences.

After she came to America, she felt alone, save for my father, then my brother and me. We weren't enough, and her hunger lunged through me.

"Don't leave me," she cried when I was ten, twenty, thirty. When she and my father moved from Brooklyn to Florida, she left me. Our relationship had been punctuated by a closeness that asked much of me. When she moved away, I breathed a sigh of relief. Shortly afterwards, she left a message on my answering machine: "It's mommy. I had three heart attacks."

My father's hold on me is silent. It is in the curve of his shoulders, the slope of his eyes, the smile that asks for permission.

"Simala," he says into my answering machine, "It's Daddy." I hear his voice and I become eight years old, the age at which he still believed I would remain forever like a wind-up doll—smiling, child-like, obedient. I disappointed him gravely. I haven't been inside a synagogue in years, date only Christian men, and have renounced marriage and motherhood altogether.

When I was a young, single woman, struggling for independence, I pushed away his palms filled with cash, the shopping bags he brought to my door filled with lamb chops and steaks from the kosher butcher. When I watched him from my window, placing the bundles back in his car, my heart broke.

One day while I was moving furniture around my apartment, the channel changer broke off my television. Not wanting to purchase a new TV, I discovered that I could use pliers to change channels. Every day my father called, and in a voice thick with anxiety, he asked, "You're still using the pliers?" to which I responded, "I'm fine Dad, how are you?"

The pliers became a bitter tango between the two of us, until I came home one day and found him standing outside my apartment building, next to a large carton, marked Magnavox. As we rode up in the elevator, the box between us, the sweet flicker of independence I knew only in spurts, gave way and I saw the father of my childhood, a man with nothing to live for but the opportunity to fix his daughter's life.

Broken only by his inability to see that I was desperate to fend for myself, I tried to cast off his pain—my legacy. I could do this only when I didn't see his smile, fragile as a child's, or hear his voice which could turn to sadness in seconds. Acutely aware of the power I held over my father's heart, I sometimes accepted the packages of food he brought to my door without my permission. His eyes glistened with pleasure—as if his value was equal only to the weight of the packages.

"Why are you so strange?" my father asks. It's 1988, and we're walking up the street in Brooklyn Heights where I live. I've just returned from San Diego, where I spent two weeks looking for a job in publishing, the industry I've been working in for the past few years.

Three thousand miles felt too far from home. I flew back on the wings of fear—a girl still trying to become a woman, searching for my rightful place, a place my father can understand.

All his nieces and nephews are married and have children.

They visit their parents often, accept their gifts of money and food, and give meaning and definition to their parents' lives. I'm divorced and childless with a career as jagged as his scar. The best I can offer is that I'm a nice person. My brother has been back from Israel for many years and like my cousins, willingly accepts my parent's gifts. I don't understand how he doesn't lose his identity in the packages.

My father has arrived at my apartment unannounced, and although this upsets me, I'm unable to turn away this man whose eyes blink rapidly when he gets nervous, and who apologizes when we walk, and he bumps into a tree. I live with a foot in two worlds. When my American side takes over I'm a California girl— wind tousling my hair, salt water shimmering off my skin— the surfer girl the Beach Boys sing about. The *shtetl* sneaks into me through my father's packages.

"Why am I so strange?" I wonder, watching my father look at me as if I'm someone he met only yesterday. He takes out a stick of Wrigley's and drops the wrapper to the ground. I've developed a social conscience, and it shames me that he does this. Therapy, the woman's movement—help me to know what *I* think, what *I* want. The new world carries me far from my childhood lessons that I become a *balabatish* [wholesome] wife. To my father I'm an anomaly. What he doesn't know is that I'm an anomaly to myself as well.

Digging my hands deep into my pockets, groping for an answer that is not yet accessible, I meet his silence with my own. We're containers of secrets my father and I. I've never told him of the hurt I still carry, that years before, when he discovered I loved a man who was a non-Jew, his rejection of me was total.

His anger cutting through me, sent me running from his home, believing we would never again speak. Hitler happened so many years ago, and yet he stalks us. I understand my father's inability to contain a world where Jews and gentiles mix blood, but can he understand my need to accept love where I find it?

Watching him now, inching up the corridor grasping onto his walker, my hips nearly cave, imagining the plastic implements, that have become part of his body. What is it like to be unable to rely on the power of the body alone to get from one side of the room to another?

I see my father forty years ago, leaning into the newspaper, weakness etched into his silhouette, and I wonder—was it just a shadow of my own design? Was it his fragility I saw, or my own inability to turn back time, to undo the works of Hitler? I love my father, perhaps, more than I love myself, but can I ever forgive him for trying to hold on to some scrap of yesterday, when it nearly defeated my own purposes to get on with my life? He smiles, and I go weak.

When I was a young girl my father and I were infamous pals. We sat together for hours separated by a checkerboard, the television set's hum the only sound in the room. So full in its simplicity, it was a time of grace. For each other, we were enough. Now, through the distance of time and miles, the ghosts of who we wish the other had become, still shadow us. I harbor a wish for a Dad who can heal me. He longs for a daughter who can ask for help.

Motherhood—Not Always A Clear Choice
(or, the baby issue #3)

It's one of those great days when everything I do clicks. I've just put the finishing touches on an article, set up an interview for a job I really want, and found the perfect dress in the back of my closet for tonight's blind date.

Sun streams into my living room and forms an umbrella of light over my plants. The day sparkles. I want for nothing and feel deeply that I will never have regret for as long as I live. I turn off my computer, reward myself with a trip to the health club and take the steps up to it two at a time. Walking inside, I bump into my friend Linda who is on her way out, pushing her three-year-old Robert in the stroller. Is it my imagination or is every woman here either pregnant or attending a mommy and me class?

"Sandy," Robert calls. He spreads his arms wide for a major hug. In his red corduroy overalls he's sending love vibrations as soft as silk and plants a wet kiss on my cheek. My contentment with my life flashes before my eyes, and I ask myself the question I continually believe I've put to rest. "Is it really OK with me to be forever the "aunt" and not the "mom?"

Before Robert was born, one of the things Linda and I had in common was that we were both entering our 40s childless. She was newly married, wanted to be a mother and felt a sense of urgency about it. But her husband, already the father of two from a previous marriage, wasn't sure he wanted to start another family. There she was—married, a strong desire to have a baby, but having to wait for someone else's time clock to catch up to hers.

For me the scenario had played out differently. Even though I went through stages in which I longed for children, the pieces of my life were never quite in place for that to happen. In my mid-thirties, when women of my generation were being told that we could have it all, I made myself a promise: if a man who wanted a family didn't show up by the time I was 40, I would do whatever it took even if it meant being a single mom.

But when I turned 40 I experienced a freedom that I hadn't ever felt before. The "shoulds" that my family and society had placed on me—marriage, family, career, material success—were things I looked at from a new perspective. My entire life wasn't ahead of me, and I wanted to enjoy it without worrying about fulfilling a requirement that wasn't readily forthcoming.

Part of the difficulty has been that my feelings constantly change. In my early forties I was involved with a man who was already a father. He told me from the start, he had no interest in starting a new family. I enjoyed what that relationship had to offer without expecting anything to change. Just when I believed the "baby" issue was put to rest, I met Richard, a seemingly loving man who wanted to have a child. As we began dating, my maternal instincts came rushing to the forefront, but then he died suddenly. I was 44. The clock was no longer ticking. The alarm was ringing full blast.

At the same time, I became more focused on my career, and was enjoying the success that tending to my work brought me. As I slid into 45, the words *last chance,* blinked before me like neon lights. I questioned daily if I'd be able to live happily without being a mother. Although I wasn't sure, I took no steps to make that happen, and spent almost all of my time at the keyboard. I don't know when I began to equate the writing of the book I'm working on with that of nurturing a child, but I've started to feel a mental "fertility" that comes without a clock attached. This could be my first "adult-sized" goal for which time isn't running out.

Still, I often feel something tugging at me, as if something has been left undone. I've identified myself for so long as not just a woman who would one day bear children, but also as a woman pursuing someone with whom to make that happen. Giving up the dream also means giving up the chase. As my life becomes just about living, I feel as if I'm getting a crack at 20 again, unburdened. But I also feel as if something so paramount to my being is missing, that I ask myself, "What am I not worrying about that I should be?" Without the panic and stress of trying to attain the elusive, I'm both grieving for what will never be and ever so grateful that the gig is up.

I finally let Robert go and carry his touch with me into my Broadway Jazz class. I kick up a storm in the front row, imagining myself starring in *A Chorus Line*—the Ann Reinking role, of course. The music infuses and frees me, and I think again about the open road I'm traveling. My eyes well up, acknowledging that some of the things I once wanted aren't on it. But some things lie on that road I never ever dared to want.

"Do you want children?" the man I'm out on a date with asks.

"No way," I say, surprised at the vehemence with which the words fall from my lips, enjoying the sound of them so much I want to swallow them up and hear them again.

No way, echoes so loud in my brain, I almost miss his words, "I don't either."

This is such a great day. Not because my date and I are in sync. I'm just so glad I went first. No hesitation, no wondering, Are you the one? Will you be the father of my child?

He smiles. I smile back. The stakes are low, and I feel good. So good that I want to turn around and look for what's missing. But I squelch the urge because I already know. There are no mommy and daddy shadows lurking.

It's just dinner for two.

Raising The Bar For Mr. Right

He has a great face. A longish nose, soft brown eyes that look right at you, full lips, his high forehead shadowed by the visor on his baseball cap.

Stats: Age, 52. Marital Status, Divorced. Children, 2. Religion, None.

Welcome to my world of Internet dating. Out of the numerous online dating services clogging up the cyberwaves, I remain faithful to a service for singles of all denominations. Even though I have strong Jewish roots, the partner of my dreams is a nice non-Jewish guy. A man whose background is my complete opposite, is who I want. At least this is what I like to believe.

Case in point: I log on to the Web site, set up a search, plug in qualities that are important to me, like the right age, marital status, education, and then voilá! Hundreds of thumbnail photos appear with tag lines ("Down-to-earth guy seeks normal woman..."), one among them, Mr. Great Face, a.k.a. Sleepless-in-NY_2,318. He looks Jewish, which appeals to me, in spite of myself. I shoot him an e-mail.

"Hi. Sleepless, your photo and profile intrigue me. I hope to hear from you. Regards, Sandy (citygirl_14,185)."

"Hey Sandy, you're pretty. Thanks for writing. I'm in New Paltz. Do you know how hard it is to get a half-sour pickle here? By the way, do you keep kosher? Shalom, Dave."

"Hi Dave, thanks for your nice note. You must be observant since you ask if I keep kosher. You should know upfront that I'm a lapsed Jew. I don't think we're a match. But, I, too, can appreciate

*a good half-sour pickle. I hope you find one soon. Regards,
Sandy"*

*"Dear Sandy, I asked if you're kosher because you checked
off that you're Jewish.   My thinking was that if you're observant
then we are not, as you put it, a match. As for religion, I'm an
atheist. I believe in peace and mercy. If you'd like to talk, here's
my phone number. If not, may you walk in love and be sheltered
from harm. Dave"*

(Time out to consider the situation…decide to call him up.
Walking in love sounds pretty kosher.) "Hi." (Awkward pause.)
"Is this Dave?"

"Yeah?"

"This is Sandy…citygirl?"

"That was fast."

"I think it's good to talk before building up expectations."

"Okay, what would you like to know about me?"

"Well, what are you going to do about your sour-pickle
situation?"

(He laughs.) "I have a guest room. You can visit me and
bring some with you."

"I love New Paltz. Don't a lot of Jews live there?"
(Notice: I have ignored Dave's "visit me" cue.)

"Yes. But you can't get any good pickles. When I lived in
Brooklyn with my *shiksa* wife, we had great delicatessens. But
she didn't get it about half-sour pickles."

"Is that why you divorced?"

"We divorced because she's insane! I even converted to
Catholicism for her."

"You're Jewish and converted?"

"I was born Jewish. When I married a *shiksa* my parents
disowned me. What does that say about Jews?"

"Well, it says something about your parents…I don't
know about…"

"…I have two daughters they never met."

"That's sad."

"Sad? Sandy, this is sad. No one told me when my mother
was dying…they didn't want a *goy* at her funeral."

(I'm so glad I hit *67 and blocked my phone number.)

"Well, when you divorced did you convert back?"

"Why would I do that?"

(Pause to ask myself, am I upset that he gave up his Jewishness or because he is Mr. Red Flag?) "Well it sounds like you became Catholic because you're angry at your parents." (I hate when I sound like a shrink.)

"Sandy, why did you get so uptight when I asked if you were kosher?"

"Well...I thought you were observant."

"You don't like that I was Jewish and converted—but you don't want an observant Jew either."

"I guess I'm somewhere in the middle."

"You want a regular Jewish guy."

"Or a non-Jew who is an authentic non-Jew."

"That makes no sense."

"You gave up being Jewish, Dave. That's sacrilegious."

"If you knew anything about Judaism you'd know that you can never give up your Jewishness."

"You know Dave, you're very intense. Your first e-mail was lighthearted."

"You don't like intense?"

"Well...actually I do."

"If I converted back, would that work for you?"

"I don't think so. You gave up being a Jew...that's wrong. Maybe I'm more Jewish than I realized."

"But if I convert, I'll be intensely Jewish."

"Well, the man for me may be Jewish after all, but not too Jewish."

"So what you're saying is, anyway you slice the half-sour pickle, we aren't a match."

"I'm not sure that metaphor works."

"Sandy, you're very hard to please."

Echoes Of Loss

I'm standing in the kitchen watching my mother talk on the telephone. The blue eye-shadow that covers her eyelids melts down her cheeks, and she looks like a Kabuki doll.

"Noooo," my mother wails as if she's strangling. Her hand shoots up to her throat.

"Esther is dead," she says, turning toward me, her face contorted. "She killed herself."

Esther is my mother's friend; a Holocaust survivor, too. The year is 1965, and I'm fourteen years old. Stories that begin and end with death define my life. My mother cries often; the sharp edge of her tears piercing me. Today, as she listens to the news of Esther, the timbre of her voice is dulled. Details fall from her lips as if she's reading a grocery list:

"The shock treatments didn't work. She hung herself from the shower rod. David found her when he came home from school." David, her son, is eleven years old.

The telephone takes center stage. It rings, and we make calls. My mother's voice rises and falls. Her emotions peak but seconds later she is still as a corpse staring into the distance at something I can't see. I picture Esther dangling lifelessly, and try to feel what David felt when he saw his mother dead. A morbid curiosity takes hold, so that I carry that image for months. My mother's friends come and go all week, their tears thick and hot like lava. Their gaze burns into my eyes, which are dry as sand. I'm ashamed at my inability to cry.

Today, when I think back to Esther's death, there are two things that I remember most: My mother listening on the telephone as she received the news, and the image of David that she painted for years after—that he carried his mother's picture every day in a shirt pocket close to his heart.

"David thinks about Esther every day," she'd say on more than one occasion. Fear of losing my own mother to sickness or death was so woven into the texture of my being, that I can't say when I first felt it.

Sometimes I think that she clutched her heart or took to her bed as a way of manipulating my attentions. But my mother was not contrived. Death and loss were as close to her as roommates.

"One day you'll miss me," my mother would caution, when my friends from school filled my time, and I began having my own life. If I spurned her attention, she would admonish me, "Who knows how long I'll be here?" or some variation like, "Your mother is your best friend," "As long as your mother is around," "There's no one like your mother."

My mother's words sat on my skin like a boulder that had rolled over me, slowly, carefully, pushing in on me, so that my bones eventually carried their echo. I felt her eminent loss with every movement even when I'd twist my covers around me in my sleep. She was in my wrists and elbows and knees and feet. I couldn't run away, or slap a door closed to get some privacy. Her voice quaked through me like a tremor, so that just like her mother was, my mother was the center of me.

When I got older and left her house, I found my voice and inserted it somewhere between the cartilages and arteries, and I mended to a degree. But sometimes when I'd least expect it, her need pulled me. Curled inside a gust of wind or riding the down-beat of a melody my feet were tapping to, her voice would come to me, saying, "David thinks about Esther every day." I'd stare at the telephone and shudder, fearful of its ring.

I heard long ago that David married and had kids, and al-though no one mentioned it, I'd be surprised to learn he still carries his mother's picture near his heart. That place in him has held his babies just as close, and his wife's hands and lips I would imagine. As for me, I never did cry over Esther's death, but I cried often for my mother's life, which swung before me like a pendulum.

Breaking With Tradition

The quiet envelops me like a hug in my ninth floor apartment where the sounds of traffic and crying babies don't reach. Yet it will soon be broken by a cacophony of stomps and claps and song. Simchas Torah celebrations will send men, women and children swaying and singing in front of the synagogue at my corner. Billowy skirts will flare out, and dark suited arms will stretch to reach about the shoulders of those who dance a circle around a Torah.

Each autumn, the High Holy Days of Rosh Hashanah and Yom Kippur welcome in the Jewish New Year with a period of quiet reflection. Two weeks later Simchas Torah celebrations break through the air like a thunderbolt. Jews worldwide pay homage to the Torah as they begin its yearlong ceremonial reading.

As a Jew who has spent my life shunning my roots, I'm shocked at the primal surge shooting from my belly down into my limbs in my desire to belong to this holiday's displays of ritual, custom and noise.

Yet all I do is watch.

Unraveling the layers of my memory, I see Judaism as I learned it as a child. Seated at the dinner table in our apartment in Crown Heights, my father and brother wore their yarmulkes, my brother's a tiny, crocheted circle of rayon fibers, my father's wide and satin. If the doorbell rang while we were having dinner, if it was a neighbor or friends, or sometimes a Jehovah's Witness, my father's and brother's hands would fly to their heads, removing the round caps from their hair in one movement so swift, so synchronous, like shadows of each other. A stranger to earth, an alien, would have thought that was the way men said hello on this planet, the custom. Reach atop the head and curl into a ball a cap then hide it within the palm, removing all trace.

In the privacy of our home we displayed our symbols. But outside, in our neighborhood, which was a crazy quilt of religions, we tried to assimilate, blending in with the American Jews who spoke unaccented English.

To the outside world my mother smiled. But when we were alone, while my father and brother were in synagogue, she'd bend her head down into my lap and spread her ringlets apart with her fingers. I saw the patches of bald spots, where, as a girl, she'd been hit with rocks on her way to school and called Jew, like a curse.

I sensed my father's pain in the way he smiled so that his lips spread ever so slightly, but never fully across his face, and in his self-effacing apologies. He found his voice in his prayers each morning when he stood before the windows, leaning into his prayer books and kissing the fringes of his *talis*. Swaying back and forth as if in a trance, he communed in a language that seemed to reach beyond time. The movement of his body swirled in me like a top, and I imagined his parents and four brothers rising through the mountain of dead bodies, like lava from a volcano.

When my father and brother were out at night, my mother and I sneaked out for Chinese food, although we were kosher. We sat in a corner of a darkened restaurant like spies, ordering one from column A, one from Column B, and sharing one bowl of wonton soup between us. We saved the slivers of pork for last, chewing them slowly, embedding their taste in our memory. On the way home my mother would remind me, it was our secret.

The daily rhythms of our lives were a hush. But on holidays, when all religions celebrated in full view, we did the same. Menorah candles burned in front of our windows on Chanukah so that all the neighborhood could find us. Before Passover my mother went to the market and loaded the shopping cart with so much matzo, the boxes almost toppled into the aisles. Our Jewishness was so big others could trip over it. At our Seder when my Israeli cousins joined us, we drank sweet wine and sang at the top of our lungs, our voices drunk on life and family, echoing through the courtyard.

During Rosh Hashanah and Yom Kippur my parents' jewelry store had a large sign on the door: "Closed for Religious Observance." My mother and I walked to synagogue, my gold charm bracelet clattering against my wrist. The hairs of her wool suit brushed against my arm. I felt a confusing mixture of loyalty and shame as she pressed me close, and we passed my friends, Jews among them, playing ring-o-levio on a day when God was watching.

In shul I gave thanks for my life and for my family's. Still, sadness was often closer to me than my best friend.

I grew into a young woman who hid from life, so that joy had a hard time finding me. When I left my parents' home I traced the roots of my sorrow to the stories my mother had told me and my father's silent prayers. I pulled away from my parents and from Judaism, which I saw as a language of suffering. I closed the door, too, on the celebrations which had once given me joy, not understanding why on holidays when the air was thick with tradition, I'd ache to sip sweet wine from a fluted glass, and toast the night with song.

Every year at this time, I watch from my window as a crowd dances around a Torah. I imagine myself flying down the stairs to kiss the scroll with my fingertips, and thread my fingers through those of others, announcing that I am a Jew. But instead I pull my head in from the window, telling myself, "That's silly."

Now, remembering the feel of my body straining against my will, I wonder if when Simchas Torah arrives this year, I'll break free from the confines of my ninth-floor apartment, to join the crowd as it kicks up its heels and stamps the earth with blessings.

About A Bird

During the summer of 1960 my parakeet Pokey disappeared. I was with my family in the Catskill Mountains, a summer retreat for the *greena*—greenhorns, like my parents who had emigrated from Eastern Europe. My aunt had offered to take care of Pokey for the two months we were at Friedman's bungalows. On our way to the country, we dropped him off in his cage, along with a box of seeds.

When we returned to the city, my mother telephoned my aunt Helen to say we would be over to pick up the bird. My aunt told her that while she was changing Pokey's water, he flew out the open cage door and then the living room window.

I didn't know anything about birds other than the daily care of my one Pokey. I didn't know that a house-bound parakeet would not survive in the outside.

I remember feeling sad that he was gone and angry at my aunt. I felt thwarted within these two feelings. I had no way to deal with my own sadness, no soothing mechanism. When I brought my sadness to my parents, their reactions were unpredictable. Most often my father's shoulders fell in more deeply, his face pulled downward. When I cried, he cried, too. "Don't cry, Simala," he would say.

But he could also laugh and say, *"Narishkeit"* [foolishness]. For what was a lost bird compared to what he'd experienced? He never said those words, but that was what I intuited in the shrug of his shoulders and his look of utter helplessness.

My mother might have tried to comfort me by saying, "It's

nothing, Simala, nothing." She might also have said, "Your aunt feels bad, sha!" Except if I was really suffering she would have comforted me one hundred percent. When my inner turmoil was so severe I burst into wracked sobs, she put her arms around me, told me, "Never hold it in, Simala. Just shoot it out! Whatever you feel."

But I almost never could. And I didn't that afternoon.

My parents paid little attention to me or Pokey's exit from our family. They had known captivity. Maybe they felt a visceral glee imagining him fluttering his wings, taking flight.

Or, perhaps they didn't understand the attachment that had formed between me and my bird.

One afternoon in my grown up life, I went with my cousin Vivian—my aunt Helen's daughter—to the Metropolitan Museum of Art. We spent an hour touring the paintings—mostly Impressionists. Then we went to the indoor sculpture garden for lunch. Vivian is kosher and brought a sandwich. I long ago gave up most Jewish traditions, and so I bought a cappuccino and a scone.

Vivian and I talked about her grandchildren, our mothers and silly stuff—makeup, facials, where to buy discount shoes. At some point I brought up the summer her mother had watched my parakeet.

Vivian said, "*I had* a bird. His name was Pokey!"

I was stunned. "No. Pokey was my bird! Your mother was watching him for me."

"Sandy, I know I had a bird. His name was Pokey."

Everything alive inside of me shut down. "Well…you must have gotten the name from me."

"No. That's not what happened."

I began shaking, horrified at the unfolding travesty. "What you're saying is that my bird didn't fly out the window when your mother opened the cage."

Vivian's cheeks reddened. "Are you saying my mother is a liar?"

"No," I said, although I felt, yes, somewhere there had been a lie. I was about to combust, didn't know what to do with my feelings. I didn't know how to have a heated conflict with someone I loved and have it end fairly.

We brushed the topic aside, finished lunch and took a walk

through Central Park, sitting for a while at the toy boat pond, my favorite part of the park. But I was sick inside, that Pokey had been stolen from me.

Later that day, I sent Vivian an e-mail.

-*I'm upset about Pokey.*

-*I'm upset you inferred my mother would lie,* she wrote back

-*I'm sorry,* I wrote, *But this doesn't make any sense.*

-*It's crazy to fight over a bird,"* she responded. *Look at what our parents lived through.*

-*Yes, it's crazy to fight over a bird.*

-*Ok.*

-*Ok.*

-*I love you.*

-*I love you, too.*

I tried not to think about the story of Pokey. But memories kept surfacing. I recalled the day I sat on the overstuffed club chair in our old living room, staring at him, wondering what to name my bird. He was in a rectangular metal cage that rested on a snack tray as we hadn't yet purchased a stand. He crept up the green plastic ladder to peck at his water tray. His head darted in and out, and that was why I called him Pokey.

How could Vivian have thought he was hers, I wondered for days, weeks, months. Finally, it hit me. She must not have been home the day we had dropped him off with her mother. When she came home and heard him chirping, she assumed her parents had purchased him for her. And if so, what then could her parents have said? "No, Vivala, he's Simala's not yours?"

That made perfect sense. And in that case, it was *lucky* Pokey had flown away, for what would my aunt have done? Held a knife to his tiny body and threaten to split him in half to see who hollered the loudest, "Don't hurt him!?" To see who was the real mother?

I'll never know for sure what happened to my bird.

But, what I do know is that I can never discuss Pokey with Vivian. Not if I want us to remain close—and in this case, close means not saying everything. For it is only now that I feel my childhood sadness over losing my treasured bird.

Knit One, Purl Two, Live Free

During my years as a knitaholic, I worked in three yarn stores around Manhattan simultaneously. On the Upper East Side I wrote patterns; on the Upper West Side I sold the yarns that would reproduce the newest Calvin Klein or Adrienne Vittadini; and in midtown I worked with the customers who ran in for a few minutes during lunch or between business meetings, briefcase in one hand, knitting bag in the other.

At night, finally having a chance to pick up my own needles, I'd sit on the edge of my bed unable to stop the mantra of *just one more row* from going round in my brain, finally falling asleep with the colors I was working with imprinted into my eyelids.

Wanting to take my obsession out of the closet and into the homes, drawers and shelves of others, I nurtured fantasies of having a breakout career as a knitwear designer, seeing my name hitting the pages of *Woman's Wear Daily*, designing those one-of-a kind sweaters for the latest version of those Cosby kids.

In my imaginary interviews of how I made it to the top, I would reflect back to a summer in the Catskills when I was a child, when my mother spent hours wrapping pink angora around my finger. It was there where I'd learned how to push my needles in and out of the stitches.

Sitting on a lounge chair a few feet from the swimming pool, I was mesmerized by my ability to make things. While kids floated by languorously in tire tubes, I turned out swatches that widened and narrowed haphazardly.

In summers past, the arduous task of making new friends rubbed up against my shyness like a dreaded curse. But in my knitting I found an easy companionship, one that asked for nothing more than the feel of my hands against the metal needles, clicking their tips as I fed them yarn. Every summer, my take-home treasures grew with me—from pink fuzzy hats to English tweed sweaters to 6-foot scarves, when I began having boyfriends.

My mother, too, had found a hiding place in her needles. While making a little something for me and my brother, she told me years later that we were her excuses, acceptable reasons to sit back and tune out while tending to the creative pull in her fingers. The sweaters or vests that the colorful rectangles hanging from her needles eventually became, were her secondary gain rather than the end result. Her joy was in the process—the gently rhythmic motion of her needles as she stared down life's complexities, with something to show for her efforts.

Many years later, when I entered the knitting field, it was out of rebellion against a string of unfulfilling office jobs. I'd worked in creative fields like advertising and publishing, but my secretarial positions kept me far removed from the end results. Hungry for work that would bring me close enough to touch the final product, something primal leaped out at me when I saw a "Help Wanted" sign in an artsy yarn store in midtown Manhattan.

By then, the toothpick-thin needles and fine yarns I'd worked with as a child had gained lots of competition from giant needles thick enough to stir a stew, and heavy, nubbly yarn. No longer considered just grandma's sport, knitting projects were aimed at the nouveau consumer—the one who wanted to knit a sweater in a weekend, a group to which I self-consciously subscribed.

Able to knit an entire sleeve while waiting for a train, I realized that without stopping to correct mistakes, I could knit two. Like my mother, I knit to quench the restless ache in my fingers. Unlike her, I loved the finished goods. Artfully working my mistakes into the patterns—cables twisted at the wrong row count or a dropped stitch creating its own peculiar design, gave my work personality. Instead of ripping out hours of labor when my needles ran amuck, I went with them, seeing where the error of my ways took me. Either I created the most imaginative work of wearable art, or it ended up in the giveaway bin in my closet. What a release to have found a place in my life, where mistakes were a good thing!

By then I had developed a severe case of knitting fever. But after years of running around town, piecing together a bare semblance of a living, I needed a job with a livable salary and benefits. My love for the written word made an editing job a viable choice. By day I diligently adhered to editorial-style guidelines and office practices, training myself to strive for perfection and follow rules. At night I longed to dive into my projects where it was de rigueur to toss out rules and make mistakes.

Winter, with its hot cocoa and angora scarves, seemed the perfect time to let my addiction run me. But in summer I could bypass the pricey cottons and linens, and dig through the sale bins for last season's trendiest wools, while also taking a mental trip back to childhood.

And so began a ritual, toting my yarns wherever I go (yes, even the beach) in order to welcome in autumn with a bulky cardigan, oversized mohair pullover, or just about anything with a bit of scratch to it. Working the sand and bits of shells into my sweaters, I stare at the ocean waves while clicking my needles, and with any luck, drop a stitch.

A Man, A Poem and A Candle

Ron, the man I'm dating, but who is not my boyfriend, bought two books of Billy Collins poems. I was with him at Barnes & Noble at Union Square when he bought them, which was right after we'd had dinner at Zen Palate, something with soy and another thing curried.

I remember that night so vividly, the way the pieces of that date fell together, as if I had orchestrated the event, intended for it to be an ideal date — nouveau health food, perusing the poetry section, *ooing* and *ahhing* as we paused over Dickinson and Keats, our fingertips running over the books' spines. There I was with a tall, slender man whose steel-gray hair I had earlier rearranged, flattening the pouf so that it looked more like a brush cut, and who, by the way, reads *The New Yorker* cover to cover.

I fell a little bit that night, into the wading pool of love. Up to my ankles. Not exactly risking everything and falling overboard into an ocean, getting soaked in love's holy water. But, nevertheless, I was in water. And the reason I'd gotten there was not because of the poetry books per se, or the trendy food, or *The New Yorker*.

It began with the way Ron deliberately flipped through one of the Billy Collins books he'd taken down from the shelf, until he came upon a particular poem. And that poem and the way he read it, in his rich baritone, so deep, his vocal chords seemed to reside in his toes, was the reason I lost my balance.

But first, a little background. A few weeks before our evening in the poetry section at Barnes & Noble, Ron and I had a date. After, we came back to my studio apartment. Instead of turning on the lamp by the sofa as I usually did—the one that gives off a soft, pinkish light—I turned toward the five-inch wide, ivory candle that was on my dresser, resting on a glass plate, with a book of matches nearby, just waiting for me to have an evening like this one, with a man who looks like a wasp but is Jewish, and who kisses with a slow, soft thrust of his tongue, gently prying open my mouth, a man worth looking at through the hypnotically wavy glow of a candle.

So, I lit it. Then I turned on the stereo, pulled Ron to the bed, and we lay back and listened to a Norah Jones CD, enjoying her gravelly voice and the flickering light and the whoosh of the buses outside my window, our arms and legs wrapped around one another, like branches.

After a while, a long, slow, pregnant while, Ron had to go. (This is why he's not my boyfriend.) While he dressed, I put on something small and tempting, a breezy camisole I'd picked up on sale at The Gap. I then stood in front of the dresser where the candle burned, and I blew gingerly on the flame until it was out, which was just a matter of seconds, really.

I looked at Ron and asked, "Do you think it's out?"

And he looked back at me, his mouth slightly parted, eyes questioning, as if wondering why I was asking, because we were standing in the dark.

"So, it's out," I said, but still I leaned over the dresser to flip on a light so that I could check the area around the candle, and see things more definitely than the streetlights outside allowed.

There were a handful of photographs on the dresser, and some jewelry on a small dish, and, oh God, a crocheted thing bunched up, about six inches from the candle, highly flammable.

"A spark couldn't have flown..." I trailed off, staring at the upholstered sofa against the dresser on which the candle rested. And then there were the satiny pillows lining the back of the couch, ending right where the curtain fell.

Ron shook his head and said, "No."

No. That's all. I wanted to say, are you sure? But a little voice inside said, don't. And Ron is the sort of man who knows things. He's a confirmer, you could say. And so I took the no as confirmation there would be no fire. By the time he left and I was curled in bed watching *Letterman*, the whole nonsense had passed.

So now, fast forward. Ron and I entered Barnes & Noble. I wondered as I so often do in the early stages of a relationship that isn't really a relationship, if he and I were right for each other. Really he should have been wondering that about me, after that crazy candle episode. Which, if I may segue here for a moment, was nothing compared to my cigarette episode, when I still sneaked cigarettes here and there, and was having a few puffs on my building's rooftop. I puffed hard, and an ash lit up and then flew upward. I grabbed at the air, hoping I could squash the ash, but I missed. Looking around frantically, I didn't see anything glowing and so all was more than likely, OK. But I didn't have a confirmer with me, either. And so I unwound the heavy water sprinkler we used for the rooftop garden and doused the roof.

And so, there we were at Barnes & Noble. Ron was wearing his Strand Books t-shirt and worn out jeans, which made him look boyish and nerdy and adorable. He had these two Billy Collins books in his hand. He put one down, opened *Nine Horses*, cleared his throat and began: "The Country." He smiled then, more to himself, like a chuckle. Then continued, something about a woman, a mouse, a match and a house burning down. My eyes widened, as Ron read on about the narrator's amusement over his lover's fear of fire.

I was delighted. Confirmed, you might say. There was a man who found his lover's worry lovable. Funny. Good material. And Ron was telling me that he, too, saw a flaw, and wasn't packing. I laughed from the release of it all, from my burden of being mental, sometimes. From worrying about fire which really when you think about it, isn't so bad, because fire at least is tangible.

"The candle," I whispered and Ron winked. That was when I fell.

(Note to reader: We lasted a year, the usual length of a relationship with a man who is not my boyfriend.)

WHEN THE SEDER COMES HOME

As a single woman with a strained family relationship, I've spent many Passovers looking for a place to call home.

In my quest, I've Sedered with boyfriends over candlelight, roast chicken and a token box of matzo; at a Greenwich Village yoga center chanting *om* while dipping into the horseradish; at a nondenominational Seder where three hours of prayers preceded the first course (non-Jews take note: Seders are all about food!); with friends' families where I enjoyed observing their familial dysfunctions; forgetting the whole thing by spacing out in the steam room at a spa; and last year with cousins I hadn't seen in a long time, whose table was filled with light conversation (no one asked why I'm not married), food (served quite promptly), kids arguing over the privilege of sitting next to me, and family love, a teensy bit removed. This Seder, this last, gave me hope that the Seder of my dreams is still, somewhere out there.

When I was a young girl, Passover was my favorite holiday. There was the large, gold-engraved glass filled with wine for Elijah—the table's centerpiece; the child-size glass with two painted cherries that I drank from each year; the red stain on the white damask tablecloth—at first accidental, and then a tradition so that at every Seder all eyes waited for me to jiggle my glass until a few drops of wine spread across the cloth; the prayers falling gracefully from my father's lips as he held his wine glass, davening, looking regal with his talis wrapped about his shoulders; my brother praying with him, stopping every now and then to mouth across the table to my mother, "Foooood?" And she scurrying into the kitchen to check on the numerous pots on the stove top, sending forth aromas of freshly basted turkey, breadless stuffing and matzo meal latkes, making my stomach swell with anticipation.

In 1960, when I was nine, my aunt, uncle and cousins who'd recently moved from Israel joined us for our Seder. I'd worked myself into a frenzy helping my mother set the table, running in and out of the kitchen, sneaking tastes. Nighttime, our table, which took up the entire living room, grew lush with family chattering in Hebrew, English and Yiddish, our prayers in perfect harmony, our songs in total discord. When we sang *Dayenu*, the American and Hebrew melodies widely diverged, but we sang anyway, loud and raucous, drunk on Manischewitz and love. After the Seder I sat on the sofa between my two male cousins who were a few years older than I, my head resting lazily on one's shoulder. It was one of the best nights of my life.

The following year my brother, a sullen teenager not fond of company, set down a law: he didn't want relatives at our Seder. So that year, the four of us had a Seder like all the ones that had come before. The large table was spacious. The prayers moved swiftly. Our plates overflowed with food. After dinner, my mother went to the kitchen to wash the dishes. My brother and father quietly recited the prayers after the meal. Then my father and I sang one last song, *"Echad Mi Yodea."* This was a ritual that deeply connected us. The Seder was like all that had come before 1960. But for me, something I couldn't yet put to words had forever changed.

I went to my parents' Seders into my mid-thirties, bringing various companions—boyfriends (only the Jewish ones) and friends (non-Jews were OK). Sometimes an aunt my brother liked was there. He also occasionally brought guests.

The cherry glass disappeared from our table. The story was murky—either it broke or it was lost during a move. Then one year it miraculously showed up. It embarrassed me how sad I was, a woman in her thirties, mourning for a glass, and always wanting to hear my cousins' voices, their thick Hebrew accents rich with emotion, ringing through the apartment.

For many years I'd ask my parents to accept invitations from our relatives, so that I could again hear my cousins' voices resounding in my ears. Preferring their privacy, they'd decline. Once I went without them and spent the night imagining my father singing "*Echad Mi Yodea*" by himself, picturing my empty seat at the table, feeling his loss.

Unable to find my own holiday home, I grew to dislike Passover. The supermarket aisles of kosher-for-Passover honey cakes and chocolate-covered macaroons—how they'd once made my mouth water! I'd look away while pushing my cart up the aisles, purchasing instead products made with bread. I stopped going to my parents' home, refused invitations to friends' homes afraid their Seders would make me sad, put my foot down when singles' Seders were suggested; and tried as well as I could to ignore the holiday. In a large East Coast city that's not easy. Jewish holidays get their due. People leave work early and rush to a dinner, somewhere, anywhere. I wanted to rush somewhere too.

Last December, perhaps because of September 11 and a new beau at my side, I was overcome with a desire to celebrate Chanukah. Behind the dishes I never use in a cabinet too high to reach, I located my Menorah. I prepared potato latkes. Friends came and went, and my friend Patty who is Protestant brought a dreidel not even realizing that spinning the dreidel was the tradition belonging to Chanukah. I sang a blessing over the Menorah, and Patty lit the first candle. Perhaps it was the flickering light before her face, or the heat of the candles that reddened her cheeks, but she looked as if something divine had transpired. I felt it, too.

Because the celebration was such a success, I've decided that this is my year to make a Seder. When I was a child, we didn't have large Chanukah celebrations, and so the holiday had no family history. Thus, it had been easier for me to recreate. Passover is loaded with longing—singing in discordant melodies, laughter, company, remnants of a childhood dinner, taken away while I was still hungry.

The Seder of my dreams. Is it out there? I'll need to borrow dishes, silverware, glasses, Hagaddahs. My oven is quirky so we'll have potluck. It won't be easy, but surely not as hard as staying stuck in a memory. Not nearly as interesting either.

Picturing the night ahead, I see nine men and women sitting Buddha style on my living room rug, feasting on casseroles, matzo and red wine, trying not to tip over Elijah's glass.

Patty said she's bringing a *dreidel* again. I believe we're set.

Happiness No Longer In My Own Backyard

In New York City, post-9/11 life is moving on. Anthrax aside (does that sound as strange as I think?), the news is getting a little more uplifting, with stories about World Trade Center survivors and reunions with firefighters and police officers who rescued them.

But there's a loss still felt by all of us, and quite likely for all of us this loss is different. For me, I can't stop missing all that lower Manhattan represented. I live in Brooklyn Heights in a 12-story apartment building, and the Brooklyn Bridge is a short walk from my home. It was once my staircase leading to my backyard, known as the World Financial Center. I'd go there on weekends during the summer.

This was my routine: walk over the bridge, check out J&R Music, then walk across City Hall Park down to Vesey Street. There, I'd get a hot dog (grilled, kosher, delicious!) from the vendor who dug deep into his icebox for an icy, cold diet Coke. Then, on to the marina, where I pulled a table and chair close up to the railing so I could put up my feet. I ate, wrote in my journal and watched the boats and people. It was better than a day at the Hamptons.

When I'd had my fill, I'd walk over to Borders Bookstore at the North Tower to read the magazines and browse the bookshelves. Then, of course, it was over to Century 21 Department Store for the best buys in linens even though I rarely bought anything. I simply loved looking at the comforters and duvets. When I was finished, it was back over the bridge, snapping photos for tourists posing in front of the skyline. All in all, it was a truly great afternoon.

Lower Manhattan was my favorite part of the city. I loved loving downtown, because that made me different. Most people I know tend toward the Upper West Side, or Soho, the trendy areas. To me, downtown was a world with energy all its own. No airs, no frills, just regular people going to work, wending their way through the crowded streets.

I used to walk the Brooklyn Bridge every day, except from December to March. It's safe to say I walked the bridge at least 2,000 times. Since September 11, I've walked the one-mile stretch over the East River ten times, and only because I forced myself. Sort of like getting back on the horse after having been thrown.

It feels superficial to grieve for a piece of geography when so much more was lost. But then, geography is alive too. Not in the way people are, just alive with history and all it represents. For me, even though I live dollar-to-dollar, the World Financial Center was an extension of my home. So many of the people who swarmed its buildings were like me—real people earning a living. And the Brooklynites, well, they were just happy to be working so close to home.

Much of Brooklyn's greatness derives from the famous people who were born there: Mary Tyler Moore. Barbra Streisand. Woody Allen, to name a few. I grew up in Brooklyn, and what made this borough great for me were the numerous friends I had. Yet when we get together at reunions, it's the places we reminisce about. Packman's Candy Store. Dubrow's Cafeteria. The Fox Theater. And though these places no longer exist, it was us who moved away and left them first.

My backyard is no more—at least as I once knew it. Now, it's a massive construction site/cemetery known as Ground Zero. For those who live in New York City and don't work or live near downtown, it's possible never to come in contact with this destruction. But vestiges live in every part of the city—the empty restaurants in Chinatown and Little Italy, the noxious odor when the wind is particularly strong, sweeping all the way to Park Slope, and all the memorials.

Amid the rumble of Grand Central Station, along the wall of

St. Vincent's hospital in Greenwich Village, on trees and door-ways in every neighborhood—the rubble of the World Trade Center appears in the form of frail, uncensored pleas for help. Tears sting my eyes each time I stare, memorizing every face.

Like all Americans, I wish I'd had some warning so I could have done something, take actions more important than merely "becoming patriotic" and "re-examining my priorities." Maybe even if I had known, I could've done nothing more than kiss the Bridge with my toes the last time I walked over on my way to what was once the World Financial Center. Nothing more than burn the view into my mind's eye, appreciating every second of my picnic at the marina, my stroll through Borders, my non-shopping spree through Century 21.

I've been to Ground Zero many times. I have no choice. It's my duty to look even though what I see repels me. Somewhere in there is my backyard. And this is the only way I know to give it the honor and respect it deserves.

Called By The Music

Every summer major cities around the country bring ballroom dancing outdoors. Those who are unswayed by the sweltering heat or the crowds get into the swing and prove they aren't too hot to boogie.

As a woman mingling among others looking for friendship, fun and romance, I've brought my appetites to the ballroom dancing scene. Every summer I've attended dances under the stars, trying numerous variations on a theme. With a date. With friends. Alone, although casually dating someone who was there, too. (A torturous experience.) Totally alone. (Risky, but sometimes rewarding.) I hate to admit this, but the most fun I've had is when I've been with a date because that saved me from peering into the faces showing up summer after summer—older and wearier—but like me, still hungry.

Most people for whom dancing is a way of life claim to be at these dance venues for only one reason: Dancing. Women, snugly contented in clingy dresses that ride up their thighs, tell me, "I never come here to meet men." The men, in long-sleeved shirts and dark trousers that make my arms and legs sweat, say much the same about the whole dance thing: "I treat it light. It's a little intimacy with minimum commitment."

Case in point: While dancing with a man, as soon as the music changes from a swing tune to a romantic slow dance, his body grinds up against mine. His sweat drips down my neck and his breath, hot and moist, cups my ear. Just when I'm wondering if what we're doing requires a condom, the beat kicks up again and the man says, "Thanks for the dance," and splits.

Wearing my heart on my sleeveless dress when I go out dancing is like tossing it on the ground and inviting 500 strangers to do the cha-cha on it. But I can't help myself.

Hard as I try to keep my needs in check, they dart out of my resistance as soon as my hips start swaying and skin meets skin. There's an electricity about dancing on a hot summer night in a minuscule dress that makes even the men I've rejected look incredible against the backdrop of my desire.

A few years ago, I met a wonderful man while dancing. He died not long afterward. I wrote an essay about our short-lived flirtation with romance, and that made me somewhat of a dating guru around the dance world. Dancers hanging back on the side waiting to be asked, understood my desire to find love. They let down their hair and fessed up.

"Of course that's always there, that want," one woman told me. Wearing a flared red dress with a low vee, she was sitting out her first dance of the night. Just as an arm reached between us, asking her to dance, she added, "I just don't expect to find love here."

I do. I look for it in every pair of shoes that tap up against mine. The filtering process takes place too. That's when the brain steps in and cools the body.

To outsiders looking in—couples who pass by on their way to dinner or out-of- towners in neat family bonds—bodies swirling before their eyes appear to be absolute magic. Flash bulbs pop and video cams roll. Is there anything more wholesome than dancing outdoors?

Well… some people dance with the women and men they know from the dance scene because there's safety in numbers, while attempting to look into other possibilities. Others try shielding present beaus from meeting former ones or from the potential dates whose phone numbers they're tucking away in their pocket or shoe.

"It's exhausting," says one friend. "Sometimes I want to stay at home with the air conditioner on and watch television. But the music calls to me. Maybe I like the thrill of getting out alive."

Calisthenics Anyone?

After a long hiatus, I decided to rejoin my local gym. No stranger to exercise, I've huffed and puffed at some of my city's finest. But a few years ago, my favorite stretch class instructor incorporated the use of assorted gadgetry into her routine. With that came the end of an era I had long known and loved—no frills exercise.

As an adolescent in the sixties, I worked out the only way a girl could—through the sheer force and movement of my body. The only weights I knew of were the barbells that lived under my brother's bed that occasionally mingled with the sweat of his palms. While he relied on a prop to build his macho image, I used imagination and ingenuity, borrowing from various disciplines to build a routine.

With *Sixteen Magazine* as my personal trainer, I mapped out a plan to work on my stomach, waist and legs, and paid special attention my trouble spots—skinny calves and a rear end that stuck out too prominently. For my calves, I walked back and forth in my room on my toes, 50 times. My straight up-and-down legs developed muscular curves. My other problem area also required me to walk back and forth, but on my butt. While watching television, I worked my behind and my legs as I traveled from one side of the room to the other.

What a sight I must've been. But I learned an invaluable lesson: not to take myself too seriously as I sculpted and redefined, something the exercise mavens of today seem to have lost sight of.

When I recently revisited my old stretch class, I sat down

on my mat, waiting for class to begin. With curiosity I eyeballed the crowd forming at the back of the gym and watched them select their gear – weights: 3, 5, and 10 pound; resistance bands: green for medium intensity and purple for greater resistance; a slide and steps for building a platform to place one leg up on while leaning over to work biceps and triceps; a balance ball large as a beach ball for sit-ups. The same class that once combined isometrics, dance movements and calisthenics to tone and build muscle brought new meaning to the word, *accessorize.*

I nixed the bands in favor of providing my own resistance, and the slide and steps were too scary to consider. I did, however, give in to using weights, and I admit, I liked them. A difference in my upper arms showed up that evening. On the down side, I felt more prone to injury and conscious of aches in my arms I never felt P.W. (Pre-Weight), as well as stress in my lower back.

I do know that when used properly, weights can be beneficial in many ways. That aside, I don't think each workout session should be devoted to building muscle as fast as possible, no matter how strengthened and toned my muscles become. Using nothing but my body to work out with feels like I'm creating art. It's a meditative and concentrated process where I feel more in control of my movements, less pain and stress, and most appreciatively after a day at the office, less competitive.

I could try yoga, tai chi, or pilates, all disciplines that rely on body and mind alone. But that's not what I'm looking for. I want to warm up to Madonna, stretch to Whitney, cool down to Aretha. When I'm in class I want to move to the beat without stopping to change weights, pick up other paraphernalia, switch again, and so on.

I've been to other gyms, and I've come up against the same problem. At two clubs I had to reserve my spot on the floor in advance, eliminating the spontaneity of stepping into the arena and seeing where I was most comfortable.

Call me old-fashioned, but I don't think working out should be all about work, and I shouldn't have to break a sweat just getting my equipment in gear. Of course, there's one gizmo I couldn't do without – my trusty mat. While sitting out a few bends and twists, I dream about the good old days when determination took me a long way.

Can A Jewish Girl Let Go Of Suffering?

In the early 1990s, researchers at New York's Mount Sinai hospital began studying Post Traumatic Stress Disorder (PTSD) as it related to Holocaust families. Their findings showed that the offspring of survivors experienced a more exaggerated degree of stress than their peers who had no direct tie to the Holocaust.

I decided to take a test the researchers were offering to determine if I had a deficiency of cortisol, a hormone that helps people deal with stress. However, halfway through the interview I bolted out the door, terrified that in telling personal details about my family something awful would happen.

Soon after, this same fear stared me down when I published "A Daughter's Legacy." I was so certain a Nazi living in New York would seek me out to kill me, I almost pulled the article. For weeks after it was published, each time I walked into my apartment building I clenched my shoulders imagining a bullet flying toward me.

I continued writing about the subject though, and my fear lessened. Although I had run away from the program at Mount Sinai, I was helped by the sheer knowledge that my chronic anxiety and worry appeared attributable (at least to some degree) to genetic makeup and/or the life experience I was born into. But this knowledge didn't cure me of the worry sickness.

After not getting a job I very much wanted, I blamed myself mercilessly—even though I'd done nothing wrong. I just didn't get the job. For the next month each session with my therapist was filled with "should haves." The lost job was also all I talked to my friends about, until that brought forth tales of other losses—mine and the tragedies of the world.

One friend termed me, "Our official mourner."

At times I'd get a flash of insight about my thought process. It seemed that I needed something to feel anxious about, so that removing stressful situations didn't help. My brain always discovered (or invented) something to worry about. I often said offhandedly that I had a Nazi living in my brain, terrorizing me.

After much wavering about taking psychotropic drugs, I sought pharmaceutical relief. I then began a lengthy and uncomfortable process of trial and error with different drugs and combinations. At that time, television commercials touting psychotropic drugs were yet to hit the airwaves, and I felt somewhat like a pariah.

When I see the advertisements today, I think people are getting the wrong message. *Anxiety? Phobias? Sadness lasting more than six months? You too can laugh, lift your children in the air, dance on the beach.* What they don't tell you is that genetic make-up accounts for how a particular drug will affect a particular individual. One man's dark cloud lifted on Drug A, was my insomnia and weight loss on the same drug. A woman's panic disappearing on Drug B, was my breast pain on the same medication. In addition to the side effects, what I had working against me was a deep attachment to emotional pain, making my drug trial an ambivalent journey.

Six months into this journey, I began a new course of medication, described to me by one pharmacist as "a strange drug." I was at a dance club when I took the blue capsule. I had an instinct that the drug would help me, and so as I swallowed it I felt as giddy as if I was having a cocktail. A half hour later I felt dizzy but mostly good. Within a few days a part of myself had slipped away—the suffering part.

I recall one particular day about a month later. It was a warm, summer morning, and I was walking along the East River. The sun was reflecting off the river, cutting sharp strokes through the ripples in the water. I thought to myself: *This is gorgeous. I'm so lucky to be alive!* Day after day, the same inner thoughts. *Who knew life was this good?*

When I saw my doctor, I said, "I feel as if I have amnesia because I can't recall anything upsetting."

He wasn't crazy about the amnesia part, but was delighted that I had no inclination to stay home and worry.

I'd often wondered what I'd think about if I didn't agonize about yesterday, last week, last year. The thought puzzled me. And then I found out. I thought about whatever was in front of me. Trees. Children playing. The movie I was watching. The present moment.

Along with feeling so different came a shift in the way my friends experienced me. I thought they'd be relieved that conversations no longer dragged into long, painful sagas. Two friends surprised me. One night over dinner with a close friend, I said, "Isn't it amazing? I don't worry over every little thing. Do you notice a difference in me?"

"I do," she said, sounding very serious. "I'm happy for you, and I'll support anything that's good for you." Then she leaned over the table and said quietly, "But I like you better the other way. You were more…you."

I didn't know how to respond. She was saying a good thing. I was fine the way I *really* was. But yet, I was both people—the happy, more relaxed me felt very real.

A few days later another friend put it like this: "You've become boring."

I truly loved *boring*. But a part of me must have not. Soon after, troubling side effects set in. I couldn't be out in the sun, even for a few minutes. I developed itching all over my body and a rash. Then came drowsiness and the loss of my libido.

I tapered the drug, but the side effects didn't go away. With my doctor's advice, I went off completely with the hope we'd find something else. The medicine didn't leave my system for a long time. I believed I was cured.

What a shock when I was composing an e-mail one day and became overly concerned with every word. My e-mail program unfortunately allowed me to hit "send" and then "cancel" so that I could stop the e-mails en-route. Which I did for an hour.

When I realized my sickness was back, I took my fingers off the keyboard and cried.

That was years ago, and my relationship to drug therapy continues to be ambivalent. I try something else, feel the peace that I can't conjure on my own. Then, for some reason—and there's always some reason—I go off. Mostly, I get curious about what I'm really like because I forget. At a deeper level, I can't help but wonder, do I miss the suffering? Why do I need to check in and remember?

I think about the study at Mount Sinai, the desire on the part of researchers to learn about and help those of us who were born into a world of loss and suffering. This tells me that while I was born into that world, I don't have to accept it as my legacy.

I recall my large extended family—survivors all—at weddings and bar-mitzvahs. What joyous dancing, with our hearts. We laughed and we cried, spinning circles around the bride or the bar-mitzvah boy, looping our arms through one another's. Happiness was pervasive.

But on a day-to-day level, so elusive. One day on. One day off. That wavy line became engraved in me. Changing that inscription is what I'm up against.

It's a safe bet I'll keep tampering with medication, until I decide on which side of that wavy line, lies the real me.

What's a Knitting Store Without a Yenta?

During a recent walk through Manhattan's Lower East Side, I was intent on visiting my old haunt from my knitting days, Sunray Yarn. But instead of finding a wonderfully tacky window display, where natural fibers and acrylics competed for space, I was met by a metal gate and a man standing nearby who said, "They've gone wholesale only."

In the days when I was addicted to knitting, a stop at Sunray was as necessary as blintzes at Ratner's in order to feel I'd had the complete Lower East Side experience. Unlike the yarn stores on the Upper West and East Sides that catered to trendy and upscale knitters, Sunray was my way of getting real about knitting. Sure, I bumped shoulders with those who came to purchase yarns at bargain prices, wanting to replicate the designers' latest.

But mostly, Sunray was down-home yenta: Utica Avenue—the main shopping thoroughfare I'd grown up near—with just a touch of Fifth. Sales people with names like Rose and Ida called me "sweetheart." All the while they re-sized a pattern in the time it took to say Adrienne Vittadini.

In Crown Heights I'd lived in an apartment building where the neighbors spent quality time in each other's kitchens.

"Don't talk to the yentas," my mother would tell me whenever she caught me spilling secrets, snubbing her nose at what she considered their mindless chatter. Instead of getting friendly with the mah-jongg ladies for a weekly game, my mother got knitting. She created an endless array of garments for me and my brother, argyle sweaters that hung from her needles with bobbins swaying with each stitch, jackets with zippers and linings, and ponchos with braided fringes.   With all the accessories these items required, I never sat on a misplaced needle or spotted hairs from balls of angora floating in the air. My mother loved to knit. But she was neat and no nonsense. When she was finished with her day's work, all her supplies were put away so that there wasn't a shred (or needle point!) of evidence.

And when it came to shopping for yarn—she'd make her selection and leave. No talking with the knitting ladies about a mohair blend or English tweed. No fondling, sniffing or staring into the bins. And absolutely no yentaing.

Not like me. My mother taught me and my best friend to knit when we were eight years old. The two of us would sit on folding chairs in front of my apartment building, working our fingers, elbows and mouths at a fevered pitch. Eventually other kids joined us working on lanyards and horse reins, and we formed a large semi-circle of chairs.

"Look at the little yentas," neighbors would say laughing as they watched us, their heads bobbing out of their windows.

When we left Crown Heights for a neighborhood where young and old didn't congregate outdoors, knitting became a more solitary activity. I'd sit under the hair dryer P.B. (Pre-blower days) and create scarves for my father, brother and boyfriend. Like my mother, I enjoyed being productive during down time, but unlike her, I craved a network of knitters—not just to yenta with, but to be around those who appreciated the sloppiness of the sport, others like me who lost needles in sofa cushions and left trails of fiber wherever they sat.

In the early 1980's my fantasy came of age. Yarn stores popped up all over Manhattan, and the phrase hand-knit replaced homemade with its image of yesterday's grandmother. Leaving my office job with its sleek desk and steel gray file cabinets, I opted to make a living in a warm, fuzzy ambiance surrounded by wool. As I maneuvered my time among three part-time jobs my passion quickly became my obsession. I formed a circle of friends from a subculture of women, women who loved—I mean lived—to knit.

Thinking I had found myself a cozy yenta-group, I hung out with my new knitting friends after work and on Sundays. While the click of our needles reminded me of my childhood crafts klatch, the talk was strictly designer. Instead of discussing the lives of others, or even our own, we'd talk Calvin. Demonstration of an intricate cable stitch would take up an entire evening's chat time, and on the subway ride home I'd take out my knitting and cleave to the warm looks of strangers.

Realizing I wasn't going to find buddies to knit, purl and kvetch with, I dug my heels into the profession and crossed the line into major league knitting. Who needed a social life when there were so many sweaters to be created? My needles became an extension of my arms, and I never left home without them. It wasn't long before I couldn't stop knitting.

Sitting on the edge of my bed way past midnight, I'd make up patterns on my needles, in the design-as-I go-method. While I went funky, my mother went Missoni. Like a one-woman factory she produced them at record speed, and the sales people at her local crafts store served her coffee and donuts while toting up the register.

"I thought you hated the yentas," I said one afternoon, eying some powder on her lower lip.

"I never said I hate them," she replied, her eyes narrowing to small slits. "Just that I don't want to be one."

"If you're referring to me, I haven't yenta'd in years."

While my mother questioned my yenta commitment, I began looking longingly at the customers who had "normal" jobs, trying to remember what it was like to go out to lunch. I'd never intended my beloved hobby to become my life. I just wanted something fun and different to do for a living. But with bags of yarn scattered all over my apartment, nine to five began to hold a renewed appeal with its built-in boundaries.

Trading in my needles for a step on the corporate ladder, I regaled my new friends with stories about knitting. They'd look at me longingly saying they wished they had it in them to chuck it all for a chance at odd schedules, work they could do with their hands while talking at the same time.

I didn't tell them that I hadn't small-talked in years. Instead I made up for lost time, yakking it up with my new friends over lunch. But back in an office, I missed the smell of sweat and sheep and the feel of angora against my cheek.

I began spending my off-work time in search of the perfect knitting store. Walking around the Lower East Side one day, I wandered into Sunray. I quickly got the lay of the land—bright lights instead of fancy overheads, low prices, comfy sales people. Rose asked if she could help me. While teaching me a new stitch she told me about her grandchildren. I told her about the promising date I'd had the night before. A passerby leaned over to admire the colors I'd gathered. Soon we were hearing about her mother-in-law. Time quickly passed.

But then, one day while doing some spring cleaning, I realized I had so many bags filled with skeins of yarn, I could shop in my own closet. I stopped browsing through Sunray, and began experimenting with other crafts projects. For awhile I made fabric hats; then hair accessories, then, writing took over my passions.

While walking about lower Manhattan one afternoon, I wended my way downtown. Standing in front of what used to be Sunray, I felt so sad. And since I hadn't been there—or knit—in years, I felt somewhat responsible.

But mostly I was nostalgic. There'd be no bags filled with yarn for me to carry home. No Rose or Ida. No idle talk. No opportunity to set the yenta in me free.

A Soaking Reign: For Some, Taking a Bath Is the Best

I've just returned from a country weekend in a house shared with friends. From the outside the house had all the amenities needed for a perfect summer retreat: wraparound porch, front and back yards, barbecue grill, a couple of mountain bikes leaning against the fence. City girl that I am, I felt as if I'd reached nirvana. Inside were three bedrooms decorated in early-19th century style (so far so good), island kitchen (excellent), one bathroom (uh-oh), a shower stall (okay) and no bathtub (bummer).

When I mentioned my disappointment to my friends, they were shocked to hear that I take baths in summer. Actually, they were rather amused that I bathe at all.

"You do know you're sitting in your own dirt," one said, her face all scrunched up as if a dead skunk lay somewhere on our—did I mention?—10 acres.

"A summer bath is an art form," I replied, trying to hold on to my dignity. But my cheeks reddened at the knowledge that I'd spilled my dirty, little secret, that I'm a "bath girl."

I grew up in a family of bathers. In the pre-war apartment building where I lived as a child, our bathroom was a renovation hoping to happen. Its perennially cold, white tile floor, pedestal sink with separate fixtures for hot and cold water, bathtub with peeling enamel on its exterior, and rusty shower head that either leaked or poured, made the room far from welcoming.

My mother could never erase the memory of the showers of Auschwitz. And so, she never adopted Americans' love for showers. Unable to turn on the water for a quick and hearty wake-me-up, she started her day with a bath. As she filled the tub, I'd watch her dip her fingers in the water in the way one tests a baby's bottle. When all systems were go—water not too hot but not warm either, clean towels resting on the sink (she preferred scratchy), her coffee finished and glass rinsed, she luxuriated in the gentleness of the water, the stillness of the room facing the back of our building, and the clean smell of ivory soap, which lingered on her skin all day.

For my father, brother and me—nightly baths were a practical response to an everyday need. But for my mother, baths were a sanctuary. She was prone to depression, and her eyes often looked haunted when she awoke. But in this quiet place where family needs didn't tug at her, she was transformed. After a bath, her eyes were bright, her skin was rosy, and she looked ready for the world. Dressed in high-heel pumps and flared shirt-waist dress, she'd say to me, "Simala, when you leave the house, you should always look like a lady."

From my mother's example, I learned how to care for myself. When I was a teenager, on Saturdays when my father was at synagogue, and my brother slept into the afternoon, I had the luxury of a long bath. By then we lived in Canarsie and had a fancy bathroom, with gleaming brass towel racks, a plush scatter rug, a marbleized toothbrush holder and soap dish. My nightly quick dip, turned into a teenage pampering routine, where I tuned out the world and inward toward myself.

By then I realized that most adults showered so I kept my baths secret. At sleepovers and when I worked as a camp counselor where there was no choice, I showered.

"That was great," I'd lie, wondering how anyone could stand those interludes of freezing while trying to get the water adjusted just right.

You'd think that when I started living alone, I'd have gone back to bathing. Not so. I was too embarrassed to run the water in the tub at 7:00 a.m., worrying what my neighbors would think. But the stress of a new apartment, new job, and dating, had me looking for a way to slow the world down, just for a while. I tried yoga, but while chanting "om" on my lunch hour, I kept thinking about what I'd eat after. Meditation? Paying attention to my breath was torture.

So I returned to my habit of a morning bath which seemed the perfect way to start my day without rushing into it. One morning I ran the water in the tub. It felt so civilized, like starting the day with a café au' lait, instead of a double espresso. On Saturday afternoons, after cleaning my apartment, a bath became a perfect way to restart the day.

Like many daughters I've rejected much of my mother's teachings. But a morning or midday bath that's restorative and sends me out the door "like a lady" holds a certain charm.

There's also nothing quite as sinful as waking up from a lazy summer nap, only to lie down again.

The Unveiling

The past few months have gone by in a blur and yet I have never known such clarity. Words are spoken. *Grief. Headstone. Unveiling.* They're meaningless, strange sounds, and yet people speak them to me without the slightest trace of irony. They're talking about my mother, and I want to yank the words from their mouths. They don't even know her. My father, it dawns on me, misses a woman not at all like the woman I miss, and yet we had bid these two women goodbye on the same day in the same awful way, and the people who came to comfort him held me in their embrace as well.

"You'll come for the unveiling," my father says, his voice rising slightly, but it isn't a question. It's just a few months after that awful day, and we're having a conversation I'm not ready for. "You'll come Sandy, you will."

I wonder how he can be so sure since the last time we were together things were troubled; my brother and I hardly speak. Yet, it was he who'd broken the news, leaving a no-frills message on my answering machine: "Mommy died." The unfamiliarity of his voice, the starkness of the message, the message itself, hurtled at me like a boulder.

"Please don't pressure me," I tell my father, and moments later my mother appears beside me, whispering in my ear, "*You don't have to go.*" There she is, my good mom, coming through for me in a pinch. I reach my hand out to touch her but draw back quickly, realizing with a dull ache, she's only an image living inside me. I see her face—the mom of my childhood, my young mom, the prettiest mom, her blue eyeshadow melting on her lids, her lips so full and thick, painted cherry red. She smiles at me and says my name, quiet, like a secret. Her breath across my ear, like hello.

This ceremonial unveiling so important to my father, seems beside the point for where else have I been the past months but at my mother's unveiling? As I lift the curtain from her face, the fabric of our past unravels daily through my fingers. The dense fog of quarrels and misunderstandings and disappointments, which kept us from each other is gone and there is only she and I. Words swim through my brain. *Auschwitz. Holocaust. Survivor.* Words from the past, which defined my mother, and me, too. Daughter of an Auschwitz survivor. That's who I was.

I remember the two of us in our apartment in Crown Heights, curled against each other. There were stories. *I saved my sisters from the Nazis. Ve froze in vinter.* Her eyes watery with the past. Then quickly she changes, and she's happy again. We're playing one potato two, Hungarian style. Bumping fists, she sings, *Etzem, petzem, picolara.* Then I'm outside and the Good Humor truck rings its bell and there she is, her head out the window tossing me fifteen cents wrapped in pink tissue. Now we're twisting around the living room to Chubby Checker. Shaking hips and arms wildly, we're shadows on the wall of two silly girls, and then we fall to our sides collapsing into a puddle of laughter.

Joel, my boyfriend from sixth grade, croons a love song beneath my window, and how my mother squeals with delight. She sends me a sly wink. I've watched and learned and she's proud that I'm her girl. I'm closer than her pockets, our bond deeper than a river of yesterdays and all the promises of tomorrow.

The dead weight of the unveiling hangs over me.

"I don't think I can go to Florida," I tell my shrink after hours, days, nights of deliberation. I've captured my mother inside me, like a genie in a bottle. My father and brother threaten to pop the cork on my memories.

"I know it'll be difficult," my therapist says, "but have you considered how you'll feel if you don't go?"

For the past month the unveiling has commandeered my sessions. There are other things to talk about: Joe, last year's ex sent me a letter.

"It's not about WHO we are," he wrote, *who* in those capital letters he uses for emphasis, "but WHAT we fall into."

He's no longer the focus of my inner life, but he pulls at me. I don't know how to tell him, not now. *This isn't a good time to take me where you are.*

Last night on the telephone with my father, his voice was soft and modulated.

"I hope you decide to come. For me." Maybe it was a trick, change of tactic to catch me off guard. I thought about plane schedules, tasted the salty air in Miami. Weeks before he'd said, "You'll be here. For mommy." I knew then that it wouldn't be for my mother at all - just a cool, hard stone, with two dates carved beneath her name.

The year she began and the year she ended.

The Accidental Writer

When I was growing up I loved writing stories, and I loved playing with dolls. At some point, I don't recall when, I gave up on the stories, but never the dream of one day having a real doll, one I could rock to sleep and teach things. I married young and hoped for the baby, but things didn't work out as expected.
I poured my sadness out by writing it down. My angst-ridden poetry taught me that putting my feelings on paper helped me feel better.

I signed up for a poetry class at The New School. The pen in my hand was like coming home, even though I was twenty-seven and hadn't written creatively since childhood. Suddenly, I wanted to be a writer!

A few attempts to write travel essays fell short—literally. I couldn't stick with them long enough to complete them. Perhaps I didn't yet understand that words sometimes require coaxing. Choosing a direction not too far afield—I became an editor. During that time, I wrote an essay about a failed relationship and sent it around to a few magazines and newspapers. It was rejected. I tucked my writing aspirations away, but not the realization that writing about conflict was cathartic.

After trying my hand as an editor, then being downsized by the technical-magazine publisher I worked for, I drifted. I applied to a graduate program in counseling, and took a course in American Sign Language in order to either become a career counselor or teacher of the deaf. At the same time, I threw myself into knitting projects, temped, and substitute-taught. I was hoping... actually, praying, that one of those choices would be the answer for what to do with my life, not realizing I'd already found it.

On the Jewish New Year a few months before my whirlwind career search, a friend had invited me to attend synagogue services. I don't know what made me go, as holiday rituals made me sad. At the end of the service, the Rabbi announced that the following day, three members of the congregation would speak about what being a Jew meant to them. When I got home, I was astonished to realize that I wished I'd been asked. The idea of speaking to a crowd provoked a flood of thoughts and feelings.

For months after, I imagined standing before the congregation, talking about how I felt as a first-generation Jewish American woman. One day I sat down and began what turned into the first essay in this collection, "A Daughter's Legacy." I didn't have a computer then and wrote in two friends' homes and at my temp job, borrowing computer time wherever I could get it. I was obsessed, working with a passion I'd never felt before.

When I was finished and satisfied the essay was honest but not hurtful to anyone close, meaning my family, I sent it out to at least ten publications. What a hard line to toe, I thought as I anxiously wrote out my return address one more time; honest but not angry, honest and yet, kind, honest…to a degree.

At that time I was attending a self-help group for children of Holocaust survivors. It was called a kinship group. Everyone there had a similar problem: expressing anger to parents who'd been traumatized had been very hard for us. We were all good little boys and girls.

In "A Daughter's Legacy," I'd written about how this issue had affected every aspect of my life. I also wrote about a side of my mother I deeply admired. Her beauty, her vivaciousness, her ability to charm strangers with a smile.

After the essay was published in *The Jewish Press,* I proudly told my kinship group about my success. I brought them copies of the essay. Shortly after, a female member of the group telephoned me.

"What happened to the anger I heard at our meetings?" she asked. "Why didn't you write that?"

I was stunned and questioned my right to write. Was I still being a good girl, not writing the truth? Or could there be many truths? My feelings about my mother were complex. The emotional tide constantly shifted.

I sent the essay to my parents, somewhat concerned they would focus on how they'd hurt me. But I felt proud and in some way, vindicated. Had they thought, fifty years before, they'd not only survive but have a daughter who would write of their experience?

When they received the newspaper, they called, sobbing. "We're sorry, mamala," they said, each on a different extension. I was devastated my work had brought them pain.

A week later, my father called. He confessed that he felt bad because I'd focused on my mother and said little about him. I was heartbroken. I should've given him more space, I thought, realizing that writing could be pretty painful business.

In spite of how difficult writing was, I couldn't see doing anything else. I was accepted into the graduate counseling program I'd applied to, but decided not to go. I told my parents, "I'm a writer." They bought me my first computer and printer. Their acceptance meant everything.

I was in business...sort of. I took myself off the writing-hot seat by working on topics that weren't personal. "Eight Steps to Happiness," "Surviving a Break-up," self-help pieces, not close to the bone.

But the compulsion to write about my inner life never went away. In time, I went back to writing personal essays, deciding not to show some to my family. Then I started a novel. It was a decision made with self-protection in mind: how can I work on something meaty without hurting anyone's feelings?

Three years later, the novel still a work in progress, I decided to do what I really wanted—write a memoir—a job I'm now immersed in. The process has been satisfying but excruciating—not because of digging up memories, but because of the fear of whom I'll be hurting. Writing a lousy article is a bruise to my ego, but nothing as difficult as deforming my truth into something that doesn't make anyone feel bad.

There are many days I yearn to be back at a temp job, imagining life as a writer, but not being one.

But that's no longer possible. Writing has become my way of figuring out the world and once in a while, helping others figure it out too. Occasionally I receive letters from men and women in response to my work. They have very different family back-grounds yet relate to my separation issues, my knitting addiction, my romantic experiences. These letters give me an amazing feeling, like nothing else.

I accidentally became a writer. My written words are my voice, slightly removed from the hot, raw emotion expressed at the kinship group I'd attended. But that doesn't mean my voice isn't genuine.

When honest, my stories are both painful and healing. That's the realm I live in now.

Not a place for good little boys and girls.

Acknowledgments

Some of the essays in this collection have previously appeared in the following newspapers and magazines, whose publishers and editors I thank. On occasion, essays have been further revised, or titles changed, since their original publication:

The Baltimore Jewish Times: "At One With Herself"

The Brooklyn Heights Press: "Happiness No Longer In My Own Backyard"

The Chicago Tribune: "Motherhood—Not Always A Clear Choice"

Hadassah: "Same Life, New Context," "A Quiet Ache," "Raising The Bar For Mr. Right"

www.feminista.com: "The Accidental Writer"

The Forward: "What's A Knitting Store Without A Yenta?"

The Jewish Press: "A Daughter's Legacy"

The Jewish Week: "The Unveiling"

The Los Angeles Jewish Journal: "Paging Steven Spielberg"

Na'Amat Woman: "My Daughter/My Self"

New Age Journal: "Breaking With Tradition"

The New York Times: "Keeping Alive The Dreams of Love"

The Philadelphia Inquirer: "Pondering The Biological Clock's Tick," "Called By The Music," "Knit One, Purl Two, Live Free"

Practical Living Magazine: "Calisthenics Anyone?"

The Washington Post: "Reduced Expectations," "When The Seder Comes Home" "Playing Chase, Capturing A Heart," "A Soaking Reign: For Some, Taking A Bath Is The Best"

About the Author

Sandra Hurtes was born in Brooklyn and has lived in Manhattan since 2003. She's a craftsperson and an award-winning writer. Her hand-knit sweater designs were featured in *Family Circle's Great Ideas* and *McCall's Needlework and Crafts*. Sandra has written for *The New York Times*, *The Washington Post*, *Poets & Writers*, *Women In Judaism* and many other publications. She's taught creative nonfiction workshops in Philadelphia and Manhattan. Currently, she's at work on a memoir, *Halfway Home*.